E-baby

A Novel

Robert Martin

To Nick –
I hope you
enjoy this
Bob

This book is a work of fiction. Similarities to actual persons or events are products of the author's imagination or are used fictitiously.

ABOUT THE AUTHOR

ROBERT MARTIN is a writer and actor from Erie, PA. In addition to teaching high school English and drama, he was also a secondary guidance counselor for the Millcreek Township School District. Robert was a founding member of Tennessee Backporch, a Country/Western band, serving as bass player and vocalist for fourteen years. His theatrical credits include many roles at the Erie Playhouse. He has performed professionally at the Beck Center in Cleveland, OH, and summer stock at the Mt. Gretna Theatre near Hershey, PA. He appeared in the 2002 film, *The Mothman Prophesies.* Robert has written more than a dozen murder mysteries and Medieval Feasts which have been performed throughout Pennsylvania. *E-baby* is his first novel.

PROLOGUE

In 1980 my best friend Barry ~~best Friend~~ told me about his crazy uncle who was always coming up with get-rich-quick schemes. Barry thought his uncle, whose name I only heard mentioned that one time and never committed to memory, was obviously a genius and should be listened to without question. He had this idea that he could open a business where people would rent movies on videotape and take them home, no really, to their houses, and watch them in their own living rooms. We wasted an entire Friday evening arguing the feasibility of such a venture, commencing with stir fry at the Plymouth Tavern, Barry's favorite bar, and through countless games of The Terminator, Barry's favorite pinball game, and lots of beer, Barry's favorite beverage. It was obvious to me the more he drank the more desperately he believed if we passed up the opportunity to get in on the ground floor of his uncle's bazillion dollar idea, we would be losers for the rest of our lives. I, not being quite the drinker Barry was, maintained some sense of sanity and saw the flaws in the idiot uncle's plan.

"So let's say people actually want to see a movie so much that they drive to his store and rent it. How are they supposed to watch it?" I asked.

"Pretty soon everyone's gonna have a VCR and they can just watch the movie, take it back, and rent another one. My uncle says the cash flow will be endless as soon as it catches on." Barry chugged the last of his beer and dramatically slammed the glass down on the rickety table, knocking an overloaded ashtray to the floor.

"Watch it, Dumb-ass, you're going to burn the place down and prove once and for all that you're as stupid as your uncle," I snapped at him. This was routine. Sometime around beer number eight, our conversation degenerated into this witless, abusive banter. He staggered two steps, bent over to pick the one lit butt from the mess on the floor and stuck it in his mouth. "Really?" I asked. "You're going to smoke that right off the filthy floor? People piss all over the floor in the john three feet from here and then traipse that piss all through this place."

"You're a retard," he responded and smiled.

"No. I'm a realist. Your uncle's the retard. My friend Mark, you never met him, but I went to high school with him, bought a VCR and paid over $600 for it. I'm telling you, people aren't going to be able to afford to rent video-taped movies, which, by the way, cost a fortune themselves. Mark spent the last of his money on two movies and has to watch them over and over."

And that was Barry's free pass from me to win his case. "And that's where my uncle comes in. People will want to rent movies because they can't afford to keep buying them. It's what he's counting on," he gloated. "But he needs cash to get the whole thing started. He needs to get the place, the inventory; he'll even rent VCR's to the people who can't afford to own them."

"Do you realize how much money you're talking? I just don't see it happening. Besides, people will just wait for a movie to get shown on TV. Why would someone pay to rent *Annie Hall* when they know that if they wait a couple of years, they'll get to see it for free on their televisions?"

"I don't know. Maybe you're right," Barry said, obviously deflated. "But wouldn't it be cool if we came up with something that would actually work? I want to find something where I don't have to work forever just to afford a nice car and a decent place to live."

"Sure," I agreed. "But everyone sitting around watching movies in their living rooms is not anyone's key to some big fortune. We're smart guys. We're educated, right? We can invent the next Hula Hoop or the next Frisbee. And we won't have to share anything with your demented uncle."

I haven't seen or spoken to Barry in almost thirty years. I'd hate to think that he dropped our friendship like a hot potato over the whole movie rental thing. The truth is, I suspect it may have had a little something to do with it. It was less than a year later that video stores were popping up all over like 7-11's. Barry was moving out of state to sell insurance for a company that recruited him for a job he knew he'd hate. I even knew that he'd hate it. We were at the beginning of that weird phenomenon where you went to college with the notion of fulfilling your parents' desire to have successful children, and wound up graduating into a job market where your degree had nothing to do with what you really wanted to do in life. I ran into Barry at the Plymouth. He had dumped me as a friend and renewed ties with his old high school gang, and they were giving him a drunken sendoff.

"Good luck, man," I said, offering my hand to him. He gave me a bleary stare that seemed to accuse me of being responsible for his upcoming relocation. "You're not still pissed off at me for not investing all that money, which I didn't even have to begin with, by the way, into your uncle's video store idea. Somebody beat him to it anyway." No response. I tried again. "You know, you could have gone ahead with it by yourself. It's not like you had to wait around for me."

"Not a problem," he slurred. "I got a job with Nationwide, and they're on my fuckin' side."

"Yeah, and I hear they're sending you to Tennessee. That's really cool. It's a lot warmer there, right? And you like country music. Nashville's there. And maybe sending you away to another state is a good thing. Maybe they have a better market there. I don't know."

"Why are you being such a dick?" he asked. His posse of friends muttered and made noises with their chairs, alerting him to the fact they were ready to have his back if he needed them.

"I'm not. I just want to wish you luck. And I want you to call me when you come home to visit or for holidays, or whatever." I was starting to sound lame;

it was time to leave. "Well, see you."

Maybe it was on the uncomfortable hike from Barry's gang at the pool table to the front door of the bar when I decided that he might have been right. His uncle was obviously a genius; I just couldn't see it through my own cautious nature. Not that I ever came up with anything on my own, but I decided I would never take someone else's brainstorm too lightly. Maybe Barry and I and his uncle could have been rich and set for life. Maybe that's why so many years later when my best friend Jamie told me her idea of having a baby and selling it on eBay, I resisted the urge to burst her balloon and laugh in her face.

CHAPTER ONE – "ME"

We were entering our third year of marriage and the typical but nonetheless annoying meddling of friends and family turned from questions of "When might you build a house?" or "Why don't you get a new car?" to the inevitable "When are you going to start a family?" It was puzzling that our parents joined in with the inquisition. I don't think Rachel's parents or mine really cared if we ever had kids. They certainly wouldn't be like Hallmark Channel movie grandparents that couldn't wait to take the grandkids for a few blissful weeks or, bless their good luck, an entire summer on Golden Pond, spoil them rotten, and tearfully relinquish them when it was time to send them back home. They just felt, like most of their generation, that without children there was a void. You had to have kids to have really done it right. A marriage isn't really complete without kids who will carry on the family name. Unlike Rachel who was an only child, I had two brothers who had already cranked out kids, and so the Thomas family name was already safely guaranteed to be carried on, with or without the benefit of a product of our love.

Rachel and I didn't talk about sex too much. We were happy with our routine of Saturday nights, special occasions, and the first and last days of our vacations. Maybe if we had talked about it more we would have done it more, but we seemed to fall into our contented pattern, never questioning what seemed to work so well for us. Eventually the issue of baby-making had to be addressed. Our reply of "We'll have kids when we're ready," was sounding worn out and was not appeasing some of our more zealous baby-making friends. The truth was we had decided months earlier to give it a shot, so to speak, and try for a baby.

"Maybe you should stop wearing a condom, and we'll see what happens," Rachel had suggested.

"Yeah, I could do that," I said. Rachel had not used the pill for two years after complaining about side effects from it. I'm not exactly sure what these side effects were, but I suspect they had something to do with her periods. I never bothered to even ask her since "lady issues" was a topic I avoided ever since at age six I asked my mother what was in the box that said Tampons, and she told me I never needed to know and don't ever touch them. Besides, I didn't mind using condoms for birth control because I thought condoms were fun. In our conservative sex life, the condom was the closest thing I had to a sex toy. It didn't seem to matter though, as month after month we held our breath until her time of the month arrived. And it always did. I can't speak for Rachel, but for me I think the sense of failure was stronger than the disappointment of not having conceived. It was very possible that I just wasn't all that keen on being a parent.

"So we're leaving it in God's hands, is that it?" I asked. I think I had borrowed that expression from her aunt, a real character who obviously believed that if you didn't have the power to make something happen, then God was always standing by, happy to oblige. I always thought it sounded like a big risk. What if God was having a really bad day when you turned your problem over to Him? It seemed too chancy, like a game of Russian Roulette, only now we'll let God pull the trigger.

"Well, sure, why not leave it up to God? But there are things we can still do to help things along," she said.

"Go on. I'm listening," I said.

"Now don't get upset or anything, but I think you need to get a fertility test. I was going to wait to tell you, but my gynecologist said after my last D & C, I'm clear and ready to go, but we should hurry before my endometriosis returns...which it probably will...return, that is." She started that slight stammer that seemed to appear when she had to let me in on something I might not want to hear.

And of course, my reaction wouldn't disappoint her. My male defensiveness peaked, but she was ready for it. "So your gynecologist thinks it's me. You're like...this open field, cleared of fibroid tumors and ready to be planted, and I'm some..." I paused, unable to finish my homespun analogy.

"Farmer?" she suggested, trying to help me.

"Yeah, some farmer who..."

"Can't grow crops?"

"Okay, I think we get the point."

"Well, you started it. And that's not what I'm saying or what Dr. Agnello is saying. It's just that since I appear to be…in the clear…it's worth taking a look at other explanations."

"And now we're back to me. Oh this is great," I said. "It's always the guy. If there's a reason you're not getting pregnant, then it's a sure bet who's responsible. Nice."

"Well, it's not like my gynecologist said, 'Let's gang up on your husband, and emasculate him before dinner!' I mean, she's a professional, and she's just doing her job. She's trying to help. She said she has literally dozens of patients who are going through the same thing."

"I don't think you mean "literally." She doesn't literally have dozens," I said.

"Oh for God's sake! Just suck it up and go get the test done. I'm sure you'll do well." She doesn't like it when I use a grammar misstep to dodge an issue.

I replied, "What do you mean, 'I'll do well!'? I'm not taking the SAT or a driving test here. It's not like I need to have any certain set of skills or possess some knowledge on some subject or topic. I just need to have sperm that can swim. I hate the thought of taking a test that I can't prepare for." Suddenly the crazy thought passed through my head that even though I couldn't cram for this test, I might be able to "save up" for it. If I went in with a full reserve, maybe my score would be off the charts. At the time, it seemed logical to me that I could rig this thing. "Okay, I'll do it. But we're not having sex until I go and get this done."

Rachel had this uncanny knack of being able to

read my mind. "You're not thinking you'll have a higher count if you save up, do you? Because you won't. That's not how it works. I read a pamphlet in the gynee's office. But if you think it'll help, sure, you just keep it to yourself until after the visit."

Never one to leave well enough alone, I continued, "And, just a little something for future reference. You might want to at least pretend to be a little put off by the thought of having sex withheld." As soon as I'd said it, I realized that she had easily put herself in the spousal power position by being so nonchalant about the idea of living in the no-sex zone for awhile.

"Okay," I said quickly. "Who do I call? Dr. Lang, family doctor? Or Dr. Loesch, urologist?" I flopped each of my hands up and to the outside, as if each of my hands was holding a tiny M.D.

"Loesch," she replied.

We had met Peter Loesch and his wife a year earlier at a Christmas party at our friends Jim and Kate Hall's house. It seemed to make sense to make the appointment with Peter. I needed a urologist; he was a urologist. The thought hadn't really crossed my mind that I was going to go and possibly bare it all for someone I occasionally hung out with socially. The awkwardness of it hit home as soon as I hung up the phone after making the appointment. A week later I walked into Loesch's office not quite knowing what lie ahead. I felt it might be better to keep this on a last name basis until the visit was over. "Hey, Dr. Loesch, long time no see." Or "So, Dr. Loesch, what's new in the pee pee business?" I ran a few more ice breakers through my head while I waited inside Room 2. This kept me busy and not so nervous until I was distracted by the room itself. Tongue depressors. For some reason I hadn't expected to see tongue depressors in a urologist's office. At least not such a big jar of them. Wasn't that kind of an old fashioned way of storing medical supplies? Was I seeing a doctor who refused to change with the times and keep updated on the latest advances? Should I be looking for a diploma on the wall next to all the signs about how to make payments on the same day as the visit? The giant poster on the wall of the male and female urological system distracted me. Distraction was overtaken by the earlier sense of nervousness the more I examined the winding path through throat and kidneys and bladder and finally to the penis of the well-endowed drawing. Suddenly a new thought occurred to me. Was I going to be expected to deliver the goods right there in the office on the first visit?

Suddenly the door swung open causing me to hop down from the exam table I had been instructed to occupy. "Hi, Pete. How's it going? Peter. Peter. I bet you get that a lot. I mean people probably tease you about being a urologist and being named Peter. Ha! Well, I think it's funny. Not really funny, but, you know what I mean." To sound even more maniacal I launched immediately into my one urologist joke which sprang from some deep recess in the part of my brain that stores old jokes.

"Hey, Pete, did you hear the one about the

urologist who went to sign a hospital release form for a patient? He reached into his shirt pocket and took out a thermometer, shook his head and said, 'Shit! Some asshole has my pen!'"

Finally the doctor seized the chance to get a word in. "Hah, that's funny. Some asshole has my pen. I'll be telling that one a lot. You need to relax. Why don't you sit back down on the table and tell me what's going on with you?"

"Oh, not much. Work's the same as always. How about you?" I politely inquired.

"I meant what's going on with you....down there. No one ever makes an appointment for a social visit. Everything okay?" he said in his best bedside manner.

"Well, it's not like we've been consciously trying forever, but Rachel and I haven't been using any birth control for a pretty long time, and her lady-doctor suggested I get a sperm test," I said.

He launched into a lengthy explanation of the reproductive glands, focusing on something called my epididymis, and then rambled on about counts and motility and mobility. For some reason I found myself smiling and nodding and not paying nearly as much attention as I should have. He sounded like my mechanic at Bianchi Honda, trying to explain to me why my car repair bill was so high. Same response from me. Lots of smiling and nodding, pretending I knew all of the mechanical ins and outs of auto repair. My reverie was shaken as he suddenly handed me a plastic cup with a screw-on lid. I was instructed to go to the room at the end of the hall, make my donation in private, and hand it over to a nurse. He clapped me on the back and ushered me out of the exam room and into the hallway.

"Before you leave, Jeannie at the desk is going to give you a time to come back day after tomorrow, and we'll talk about how things look. Great to see you again," said Pete.

Out of nowhere a nurse appeared and led the way down the hall to the doorway of the donation room. She discreetly lowered her voice and told me to help myself to a magazine. I thanked her and asked her if I could use the bathroom first, mumbling something about too much coffee at breakfast. I wondered if she was as embarrassed about this as I was. Probably not. She certainly did this enough that it was routine for her. For all I knew, I was just one of a number of guys this week that she had led down the hall as step one in having his baby batter analyzed. Permission was granted for the rest room first, and she reminded me about the magazines which were hiding on the bottom shelf of a side table next to a vinyl Lazy Boy. We both knew she was not offering me a *Reader's Digest*, yet we maintained this very polite repartee, as if my sole purpose for being there that day was to relax and catch up on some reading.

Two days later I was back in the office to discover that there was an abnormality in my count. When Peter first told me my count was around seven million, I was floored. I actually was worried that maybe the problem was that I had too many swimmers. Maybe there were too many of them fighting for first place. Then he told me that the normal count should be around twenty million. It was hard to grasp such a number. It was even harder for me to believe that seven million of anything wasn't enough.

I was given a prescription for something called Clomid, a fertility drug that was supposed to boost production, as well as my own "travel mug," another sample cup that I could use ten days from now in the privacy of my own home and drop off at the ACL on Peach Street. ACL stood for Associated Clinical Laboratories, a brand new lab for blood work and all kinds of testing, but more important to me, a haven of anonymity where I could deliver the goods in a small brown paper bag. Ten days later I woke up, confident that I would do better on my retest. I ate some breakfast, showered, and before I got dressed, I had my solo session with the travel mug. I quickly folded up the brown paper bag and stuck it under my armpit as I had been instructed. On the lookout for the seventeen hundred block, I drove down Peach Street, a fairly wide, four-lane road and had a panicked feeling. Where the hell was this place? I'd lived in this town my whole life, but I wasn't sure if I should be looking for this new lab on the left or the right. To the left was an old mall, recently renovated with a cheap discount store, an EmergyCare, and some other vague properties. To the right was the Professional Building, a three story structure that housed a number of physicians and law offices. It made sense to turn into the parking lot on the right, and sure enough, right in front of the parking space I chose was the address I was looking for, 1705. I turned off the car, readjusted the paper bag securely under my armpit, and made my way into the office. I walked past the four or five people waiting in chairs, right up to the receptionist who slid a window open as I approached.

"Can I help you?" she asked.

"I'm here to drop off a sample," I said sheepishly.

She looked puzzled. "I'm sorry?"

I retrieved the paper bag from under my arm and attempted to pass it through the window. She practically recoiled but responded, "I'm not sure I understand. What kind of sample is it?"

I thought it was insensitive of her to ask such a question in such close proximity to the room of patients sitting right behind me. It might have been my imagination, but I could swear they were all leaning forward in their chairs a little bit in anticipation of my answer. Just wanting to be done with it, I muttered in a subdued, breathy voice, "Sperm."

"I'm sorry. What did you say?"

A little louder. "Sperm."

"Hmmm," she said. "I think you want to be at the ACL across the street."

"Isn't this 1705 Peach Street?" I asked.

"No, this is 1705 State Street. I know it's confusing. This is an eye doctor's office," she said matter-of-factly. At that moment I noticed she was leaning away from the bag that was being extended through her window. I quickly tucked it back under my arm, offered an apology, and made my fastest exit through the waiting room of patients, praying that I didn't know any of them. When I got to the car I glanced back at the glass door and noticed the short list of doctor's names painted in black under the heading of Ophthalmologists. The July morning sun beating on the door created the glare that must have obscured the writing from my notice when I had rushed in minutes earlier.

After dropping the bag off at the appropriate destination without incident, I went home to await the results as casually as possible. Rachel was politely quiet on the subject, knowing that my anxiety level was elevated. The very next day, a brief phone conversation with Dr. Loesch informed me that my count was up considerably, and after his recent consult with Dr. Agnello, Rachel and I would be categorized as Unexplained Infertility if there weren't results in the next couple of months. We agreed that we were happy to live with Unexplained Infertility. We were back to leaving it in God's hands which took the pressure off us mere mortals. We did make one final attempt three months later with a trip to Magee Women's Hospital in Pittsburgh to try artificial insemination. When that didn't take, it was back into God's hands, only this time for good.

Eventually Rachel's endometriosis was back with a vengeance, and Dr. Agnello told her she'd have to have one ovary removed. Down the road, a total hysterectomy was almost a certainty, but she said there was still time to try for a pregnancy with the remaining ovary. She gave us some time to discuss it. I had no clue what to say, but Rachel let me off the hook.

"I don't want to go through this twice," she said. "It just doesn't seem to me like it's meant to be. I think I'd rather just be done with it and have a total hysterectomy now."

"Whatever you want," I offered. "This is definitely affecting you more than it is me. So I just want to make sure you're not disappointed. Like she said, we could keep trying."

"No. I'm really not that upset about it, and I don't think you are either. Are you?" She had a hint of sadness in her voice that was unmistakable.

"Not at all," I said, squeezing her hand. "Who needs rug rats that have to be put through college? Not to mention we can go anywhere and do anything we want without kids to hold us back."

The more we rationalized it, the luckier we saw ourselves. This was the way it was meant to be. This is what God had decided for us when it was put in His hands. Little did I know way back then that God was the only one who knew I would someday produce one little swimmer who would burst forth to start his own little miracle of life somewhere way down the line. One little Olympic swimmer who would be known around the world someday as E-baby.

CHAPTER TWO – "JAMIE"

Jamie LaRusso graduated from high school on the same day that Rachel Thomas had her hysterectomy. Jamie had been looking forward to graduation more than anything up to this point in her life, but she was three months pregnant and carrying around that secret had taken all the joy out of graduating. Jamie had been accepted to Penn State way back in December and, until the discovery that she was having a baby, had spent every day planning the exciting details of her escape from the one-horse-town she had grown up in. There was nothing wrong with Titusville to speak of, but in her mind, there wasn't much right with it either.

She felt guilty about not telling the one person in the world who deserved to know of her "situation," her boyfriend Darrell Jernigan, baby daddy. She decided to tell him right after the graduation ceremony after a long debate in her head as to whether she would then be forced to include him in any decision making. She had mapped out her options, devoting more time to mulling these over than she had spent studying for finals. She had narrowed the options down from several that had ranged from the ridiculous to the tolerable. The final tally was four. Option one, she would marry Darrell. It would be her parents' preferred way of her dealing with this predicament. It would be the easiest fix and would make the most people happy. Except herself, of course. In her mind she viewed this option as heavily weighted on the ridiculous side of the spectrum. Darrell wasn't exactly in a position to start a family. He had no ambition of college, and odds were they would break up anyway when it was time for Jamie to pursue her higher education in State College, PA. His plan was to work as a bartender at Stool Pigeons, a popular watering hole in town. His Uncle Steve was sole owner and had promised Darrell a job, proposing that in five to ten years, he would take Darrell in as a partner when he opened another joint. It sounded like a long way off, but it gave Darrell direction and time to save up. Even more appealing, it gave him a plan that didn't include more school or moving away from home or much thought in general. He was not exactly the go-getter Jamie had pictured in her mind from the time she started fantasizing about that magical day when she would walk down the aisle with the richest, most handsome guy in town.

Option two was to have the baby on her own, but this would mean forgoing college, at least for awhile. The thought of raising a child by herself didn't bother her so much. She always smiled to herself when she thought of what her grandmother proudly liked to call her, a tough cookie. As disappointed as her parents might be with this option, she felt she didn't need their approval or their money to survive. She had yearned for a long time to finally get out of the nest. If college wasn't in the cards, she would make do with her own apartment and a job. In a way, the thought of such immediate independence seemed exciting to her and not as scary as she might have thought even a month or two earlier. Graduation was a milestone that was already making her feel more grown up.

The third option was to have the baby and put it up for adoption. This option didn't get as much attention as Jamie wasn't really sure how something like that would work. Did she need a lawyer? Was there even an adoption agency in town? She was surprised that she didn't even know if there was one. She had looked up Adoptions in the Yellow Pages only to discover that no such entry existed. It wasn't exactly the type of thing she could ask anyone about without raising suspicion. If her best friend Lorene started asking her out of the blue about how to put a baby up for adoption, she would have immediately assumed that Lorene was pregnant. Even if she managed to find out about the adoption process, how would she really feel about handing a baby over to strangers when the time came? She was pretty sure she couldn't do it. There were too many unknown variables to make this much of a viable choice.

The last option wasn't really an option at all. She had heard whispers around the halls at school of a girl in her class who had had an abortion. Jamie wasn't sure if her religious beliefs were the reason she wouldn't consider this. She went to church occasionally when her parents pressed her, and she paid enough attention to form fundamental beliefs in God, right and wrong, and the importance of being a good person. Whether or not it was a moral issue, the thought of going through an abortion triggered something deep down that stopped her cold and made her shudder every time she ran the notion through her head.

By the morning of graduation Jamie had narrowed down the options to the first two. During the valedictorian's speech she had decided to tell Darrell that he was going to be a father, but he wouldn't have to worry about it affecting his life in any way because she was going to raise their baby on her own. She might even include her recently formulated idea of moving to another town where she could avoid the inevitable constant interference of her mother and father, and Darrell could be free to go on with his life. She joined her classmates as they stood and hurled their mortarboards into the air, the blue and gold tassels making a colorful display as they first flew toward the ceiling of the gymnasium and then quickly descended. Less than a half hour later, she was engaged, her life set in stone forever.

It had happened so quickly she couldn't seem to take control of the situation as it slipped away from her. After she hugged her parents, Jamie found Darrell and pulled him off to the side of the bleachers.

"Hey, I need to talk to you about something!" she shouted, trying to be heard over the din of the school orchestra. The band members were doing their best, but all of the graduating seniors were in caps and gowns and so they were out of the mix, leaving the less experienced musicians to step up.

"Can't it wait a bit? The guys are all heading to

the cafeteria before all the decent food is gone," he explained.

"This is kind of important," she said firmly as she guided him under the bleachers a few feet. He had to duck a little bit to avoid hitting his head. "I need to tell you something, and I don't want you to get upset."

"Is this about you going off to college again? You know I'm cool with that. We've talked about this a million times. Let's get to the cookies, make nice with the parents, and then we'll go have some fun." Darrell poked his finger into her butt and then grabbed her hand to lead her out from under the bleachers.

"I'm pregnant," she said, just loud enough that only he would hear.

"What?" He just stared at her. His stunned reaction was exactly what she expected.

"Say something," she prompted.

"Well…is it mine?" Immediately he knew that it was a dumb, unnecessary, and possibly dangerous question.

"Oh my god. Are you kidding me?" She was seeing red.

"No, no, no. I didn't mean to say that. I know it is. I didn't mean that. Oh crap, I'm sorry. I didn't mean to say that. I guess I was just hoping that maybe it wasn't," he stammered.

"Oh my god, you're unbelievable."

"Shit. I didn't mean that either. I'm just, I don't know, a little freaked out. Give me a second."

Darrell turned his back to her and leaned his forehead on his forearm which he had rested against the back wall. She watched him inhale slowly and then exhale even more slowly.

"This is good," he said as he turned back to face her.

"You don't have to say that. Hear me out. This doesn't have to affect you at all. I just thought you should know," Jamie said.

He continued, "No, I mean it. This is a really good thing. I mean, I wasn't really happy about the thought of you leaving for school. And now you can stay, right? I mean, you'll stay here if you're having a baby, right? See? This is awesome. We can get married. And I know you're gonna say we don't have to, but I want to. Because I really like you, you know? I mean I love you. I definitely meant to say I love you." He was nodding in a way that made it appear he was trying at least to believe the words he was saying. She couldn't tell if the huge smile plastered on his face was from happiness or shock.

It was time to break it to him. She suddenly felt like crying and needed to get this over with before he had to be dropped from any higher up than he seemed to be right now.

"You don't understand. I don't think the right answer necessarily is to just get married. Who knows if that's right for either one of us? All through high school when I'd hear girls talking about marrying their boyfriends as soon as they could, I thought they sounded like idiots." Jamie continued to list the reasons why marriage maybe wasn't the best thing for them right now. She had gotten through the obvious points about how young they were and that they didn't have any money to speak of, when she noticed he had pretty much stopped listening and was fussing with the large, heavy aluminum band around the tassel hanging from his mortarboard.

"What are you doing?" she asked.

"Jamie LaRusso," he said, as he pried open the band with his index finger. He took her left hand and began to press and reshape the gold-colored aluminum around her finger. His nervous fumbling was the sweetest thing she had ever seen in her whole life, and it took her breath away. Now it was her turn to find the back wall for support. "Would you marry me?" he asked.

She stared at the makeshift ring for a second before answering him. "No wait!" he exclaimed. "I have to do this right." All common sense and logic she had armed herself with was quickly slipping away from under the bleachers as he knelt down and asked her again.

"Will you marry me?"

"I want to. I really do. But..." Her head was shaking slowly side to side. "Alright."

And it was done. It was that simple. As simple as getting pregnant was. Surprisingly, it wasn't even very difficult convincing their parents that they would be okay. Both sets of parents seemed to adjust to the idea of a wedding more readily once they were told about their impending grandparenthood. There no objections from the Jernigan side about them getting married in the LaRusso side's church. The ecec

wedding reception in the church social hall took place just two weeks after her graduation party. She felt embarrassed as the relatives and her parents' friends who had just celebrated her graduation, tossed yet another card into the wedding gift basket. Her only attendant, her maid of honor, was her best friend Lorene. The irony of this setup did not escape Jamie's attention. She had grown up listening to Lorene constantly talking about getting married someday and how all she wanted was the perfect wedding and to have kids. Now Lorene was the one planning to leave for school in less than two months, and Jamie was the one having a wedding although she figured no one would have exactly described it as perfect.

The day after the wedding she and Darrell both began waiting tables at Stool Pigeons until Darrell's Uncle Steve suggested after several weeks that it was time for her to get off her feet and rest up for the baby. She appreciated his concern, but she knew it was really because he thought the regulars were not entirely comfortable having a pregnant teenager delivering their burgers and beer. She finally got to spend some time fixing up the apartment they had taken just two blocks from the bar. The neighborhood she had grown up in and moved away from for the first time ever was less than five miles away. Even though there wasn't much of a "big city feel" to downtown, the noise from the traffic and the continuous stream of people walking around took some getting used to. She adapted to it very quickly. Adapting to the marriage was another story. Most of her friends left for college at the end of August, just when she was entering her seventh month. She was finally getting excited and ready to spring this miracle on everyone, and they were all leaving her behind. She knew from the start this would happen. It even passed through her head right before the vows during the small, simple wedding ceremony. The abandonment would have been completely unbearable if Lorene hadn't decided at the last minute not to go to college. It would be nice to think that she was staying because her best friend Jamie needed her now more than ever, but Jamie knew it was because Lorene wasn't really college material. Their guidance counselor had told Lorene as much, suggesting that college might be a little too ambitious for her to handle. Maybe she should think about starting smaller at Jamestown Community College, or maybe she could study to be a paralegal at Erie Business Center. Each time Lorene walked into the guidance office to have Mr. Meyers write a college recommendation or send her transcript somewhere, she left with considerably more self-doubt. The last encounter with him right before graduation pushed her over the edge.

"Have you given any more thought to the medical transcription program at Great Lakes Institute?" he asked.

"Mr. Meyers," Lorene began, "you keep suggesting all of these things, but I've already been accepted to a state school and a private one, and I'm thinking of applying to one more, Penn State, but mostly because everyone else is applying there. I really want to go to a regular four-year college."

"I know you think you want to. But we've both seen your SAT and your ACT scores. Not exactly college material, do you think?" he asked.

"Why would they accept me if I wasn't smart enough?" Lorene asked timidly.

"Two reasons," Meyers said. "First, you want to major in interior design, basically a frilly major that doesn't require any real intelligence. You need to know your colors and be able to measure things. Judging from your math scores, I'm thinking that might even be a challenge for you. Secondly, they want your parents' money, plain and simple. You're paying the same as a kid who's studying pre-med, for a major that's going to, with luck, have you selling drapes at Sears for the rest of your life. You should be filling out a Sears' application, not another college application."

Lorene related this story about Meyers to her one day when Jamie had pressed her to tell her why she had decided not to go to college. Jamie wasn't surprised. After all, this was the man who paid his lunch check at the bar on the first school in-service day that August and shook his head when he recognized her from the most recent crop of seniors. "Jamie LaRusso," he said flatly as he glanced at her pregnant belly. "Maybe you should have paid more attention in health class."

"Yeah, well that's what the teacher at school who knocked me up said." Jamie had gotten some satisfaction from the lie, knowing it would drive Mr.

Meyers crazy as he eyed with suspicion every male teacher at that afternoon's faculty meeting. It came back to haunt her though. Obviously confidentiality between herself and her guidance counselor was out the window once she graduated from high school. The phone rang one night and Dr. Geary, the principal, asked for her.

Darrell handed her the phone, covering the mouthpiece with his hand. "It's Dr. Geary," he whispered loudly. "What the hell?"

"Is this Jamie LaRusso?" the principal asked.

"No," replied Jamie. "This is Jamie Jernigan. Same person, new name. I got married this summer."

"Oh, congratulations." The relief in his voice was immediately noticeable. Then he had a disturbing thought. His mind raced to think if he had heard of any of his faculty getting married in the past three months. Certainly he would have known about something so scandalous. He had to be sure.

"I need to ask you about a very troubling bit of information that was brought to my attention recently."

Immediately Jamie knew that Meyers had opened his big yap. If Geary knew, then it was likely that the entire school knew. And if the entire school knew, it wouldn't be long before most everyone in town heard the rumor. Not that she cared. Meyers was being a jackass so she had just said it, never thinking there might be any consequences.

"Is there any truth to what you told Mr. Meyers the other day, about a certain teacher at school?" he asked.

"Not exactly. I mean I am having a baby, but I'm married to the father. Remember Darrell Jernigan? He wrestled varsity. He's the father," Jamie said.

"Well, why in God's name would you tell Mr. Geary something like....what you told him?" the principal asked.

"I don't know. Why in God's name would Mr. Geary tell my best friend Lorene that she should work at Sears for the rest of her life?"

"I don't see how the two are connected," said Geary. "I'd still like an answer."

"It's the only answer I have," said Jamie. "I have to go now. I think my water's gonna break," she lied. She hung up the phone and turned to Darrell.

"Yeah, you might hear some talk going around that you're not the father of our baby. Just don't pay any attention," she said as she threw a dishtowel to him so he could wipe up the Coke he had just spilled.

"Who would say that? Why would anyone say something so mean and stupid?" he asked.

"I'm afraid that would be me," she confessed. "I kind of said something like that to Mr. Meyers when he was in the bar for lunch the other day. He was being a jerk. It really doesn't matter. No one is going to believe that I got knocked up by some teacher at school."

"Oh, my God! Is that what people think? Why would you say that? I don't get it. I don't get you," said Darrell in disbelief.

It's funny how one little off-the-cuff comment can

cause such a ripple effect in someone's life. No one really believed or cared much about the rumor, taking it for what it was, just a rumor. Jamie and Darrell's friends thought it was just about the funniest thing they ever heard. The only one who couldn't seem to find any humor in it was Darrell. Jamie always thought it should have been laughed about and then forgotten, but every time there was any friction or disagreement between her and Darrell, he went back to it like it was still some open sore that she was responsible for. It never occurred to her that her wrestler could be so sensitive, that the thought of people even remotely thinking he was not the father of the child he was raising, was a thought that ate away at him somewhere in his subconscious. Months later, one of his old wrestling buddies had come into the bar and sometime during their conversation, his friend punched his arm and asked him why Little Darrell looked so much like Mr. Pertekis. Mr. Pertekis was their eleventh grade biology teacher who always managed to assign the seats up in the front of his classroom to the prettiest girls, or at least the ones who wore short skirts most of the time. Another time his friend Damon had told him that he never believed any of the bullshit about Jamie getting tapped by a teacher. He was convinced that it was actually the school custodian who had done the deed. Darrell laughed along with his buddies, but the truth was the teasing drove him crazy.

Only once did the irrational fear buried in Darrell's subconscious actually come out in conversation. It was right after Little Darrell's second birthday party. It had all started while they were cleaning up the dishes from the ice cream and cake. As usual, both sets of parents had disappeared immediately after the presents and cake. They never seemed very comfortable celebrating family events at Darrell and Jamie's.

"Your mom never listens to anything I ever suggest for her to buy for Little Darrell," Jamie said the second the Jernigans had closed the door behind themselves. "I mean, would it kill them to give him something that was at least the littlest bit educational?"

"They gave him fun things," countered Darrell. "They know kids like fun things. There's nothing wrong with kids having fun," he said, as he intentionally tossed the plastic cake plates noisily into the cabinet over the countertop microwave.

"Oh, don't start ranting about me being some mother who won't allow her kid to have any fun," she said. "Darrell goes to play group. I take him over to the ball park and the field all the time. He has plenty of fun."

"Thank God I know someone around here is getting to have some fun. I'll be able to sleep now." Darrell knew where this would lead, but he continued anyway. "And I wouldn't worry about your parents ever giving him anything even close to fun. Why does everything have to have "learn" in it? Learn and Spell, Learn and Say, Learn and Count. That's not fun. That's work."

"Says the guy who never even wanted to go to college." She was ready to have it out.

"Well, it's not like I even could have gone to college since I had to get married," he said. "And where do you get off saying that to me? I don't see any college diploma of yours hanging on any of our walls."

"You'd see one if I didn't have to take care of a two-year-old everyday. And his son," she said, obviously pleased with her snide dig at Darrell's maturity.

Then he said it. "You're consistent if nothing else. Still sticking to the story that Little Darrell is mine."

"You are unbelievable," said Jamie. "I can't take it anymore. How is it that you can be the only person who knows me better than anyone else, but you keep running back to the ridiculous idea that there was someone else...and may I remind you, I started that fucking rumor!" The tension had been building between them for months, mostly from Jamie feeling trapped in the house every day, and Darrell feeling trapped in the house every night.

Two weeks after the birthday party, the two-year marriage was over. Jamie and Little Darrell moved into Lorene's temporarily. It was Jamie who had volunteered to be the one to move out. She knew that she'd be okay, but she wasn't so sure about Darrell and figured he'd have a better chance of keeping it together if he at least got to stay put. He had gotten extremely quiet whenever he was around her, but when she'd walk by Stool Pigeons she would peek through the front window and see him smiling and laughing like he did two and a half years ago. Deep down she knew the truth was what she had feared from the start, that they were just too young to be successful at a marriage with an instant family.

There was never a question as to who would take Little Darrell. Jamie was the one more capable of working and taking care of an infant. Actually "more willing" would have been a more accurate way of putting it. Her new start commenced with figuring out a way to finally get to college. She was obsessed with the idea of studying art, a recent discovery about herself for which she had Little Darrell to thank. It was her little boy who insisted she paint alongside him almost every night before he had to go to bed. As she sat and painted and drew with Little Darrell, it was as if a whole new person emerged. She would clean up his paints and his supplies, put him to bed, and rush back to the table for a few more hours. The only thing worth trading sleep for was painting. It became something that consumed her. She knew she might not be able to support herself and a child by painting, but that didn't matter right now. She began shyly showing her paintings to select people, first her mother and then some of the mothers from Little Darrell's play group. Everyone who saw her work was full of encouragement. She got the same reaction from Lorene every time she would show her the latest finished work. "Oh, my God, you're so good," she'd say, and Jamie never tired of hearing it. As her confidence and passion grew, she dreamed of getting immersed in the art world in college and then someday teaching art. Slippery Rock was an affordable state school not too far away that offered a decent art major. She even had Darrell's support. The school was close enough that he could help her with Little Darrell if she ever needed him to step in. The plan was perfect. There was day care offered on campus through the education department. Granted, most of the kids were from working parents in the community, but she happily discovered that she would not be the only coed with a child in the facility.

Jamie finally got to jump through all of the hoops she had missed a couple of years ago. She applied to Slippery Rock and submitted an art portfolio. Three weeks later she found herself shaking as she tore open the envelope with the college letterhead in the return address corner. Not only had she been accepted, the school was offering her financial aid through something called the President's Grant. In addition they were offering even more assistance if she was willing to do work-study through the art department. She would find a way and the time to do it.

She found a small apartment next to campus and the plan chugged along. For the first time in a long time, Jamie felt she was on the right track. She even managed to hide her surprise when Darrell arrived one Friday afternoon to pick up Little Darrell, and she noticed an attractive girl sitting in the passenger seat of his car.

Darrell sensed Jamie's subtle change in demeanor as he approached her and began an explanation. "I hope it's alright with you. It's nothing serious, and she's really nice. I mean she's cool with me having a kid and all. I probably should have checked with you first, huh?"

"Darrell, it's fine," said Jamie. "We probably should have talked earlier about something like this happening. It's okay. We're moving on, and I think we're both doing really well. Little Darrell's all excited that you're taking him to the Pittsburgh Zoo tomorrow, so I hope that's still on." She went inside and lifted Little Darrell from in front of the television and delivered him to his father who had moved onto the top step.

"Terri, this is Jamie! Jamie, this is Terri!" he shouted indicating each of them with a head toss in the direction of the name being called. "Have fun. Paint a lot. I'll have him back Sunday night," Darrell said as he went down the steps with Little Darrell in one arm and Little Darrell's knapsack in the other.

Absentmindedly Jamie kept running her top teeth over her bottom lip, waving to them as they pulled out of the parking lot of her apartment complex. She slowly went back inside and sat down next to the telephone. She stared at the phone number that was penciled on the top page of the yellow legal pad she used to organize her life. It belonged to Bill Gaither, a fun, type A college senior in her psychology class who had been flirting with her since the first day the class met. Weeks into the semester, when he noticed her staring at his frame stretched out into the aisle of the lecture room, he sat up quickly and began writing a note which he then tossed indiscreetly onto the retractable desk top of her seat. It surprised her that he knew she was an art major. She had never told him that, but his message made it obvious that he knew. It said, "I'll let you paint me naked if you'll go out with me this weekend." After class she blushed and told him that she had a child at home who needed to be taken care of but thanks for the offer.

"Are you married?" he asked.

"No, divorced. But I'm not really ready to see anyone. I'm pretty much pulled every which way with school and work and having a kid," she said.

"Well, when you're ready, give me a call," he said. "I like smart girls. You seem to understand everything that's discussed in class. I like pretty girls, and you're that too."

She dialed the number and waited for him to answer. If Darrell was moving on, then surely it was okay for her to do so too. She had just assumed nobody in college would want to go out with someone who was already someone's mother.

Bill answered after three rings. She merely said, "It's Jamie. I'm ready." She hoped he would get the reference to their last conversation. He did immediately.

He was already committed to a party off-campus, but would she like to go with him? He could pick her up at ten and have her home after the keg was kicked. She said, "Fine."

"I deserve to have some fun," she thought. She hadn't partied in so long. She had forgotten how much fun it was to be free from work and school and a kid. Bill was what she used to imagine as the perfect guy. They did shots and laughed a lot through the entire party. She was enjoying the roomful of new drinking buddies and recognized a few of them from classes they shared. Bill even helped her into the house after he drove her home. He was the perfect gentleman and she kissed him as they leaned against the inside of her front door, cautiously at first, but then more heatedly as they stumbled backwards and sideways to the couch.

"No, wait, we can't," she said as he rolled on top of her and began tugging at her shirt.

"It's okay," he panted.

"But we hardly know each other," she argued weakly.

"We've sat across from each other three times a week all semester. I think we know each other well enough," he said, pressing down on her just in case she needed the physical pressure of him to assist her with her decision.

"I'm not on birth control," she gasped.

"Not a problem," he murmured into her hair. He reached around to his back pocket and pulled out his wallet. He grasped the lone condom from behind some folded ones and fives and flung the wallet to the floor. Jamie gave a sigh of relief. She had made the mistake of not insisting Darrell use protection and didn't want to go there again. She stopped thinking of anything but the strikingly handsome man on top of her and gave in to the sheer enjoyment of sex.

The next morning she woke up on the couch. She was conscious of smiling as she squinted from the sunbeam directly in her eyes. She took a second to stretch and get her bearings. Bill was gone, but he had placed a pillow from her bed under her head and covered her with the comforter that usually adorned the back of the couch. She thought it was sweet that he had done that for her. She threw the covering back and walked to the bathroom where she bent over the sink and took a drink of water from the faucet. She turned on the shower and started to remove the few items of clothing that she was still wearing. Her bra was on the living room floor on top of her jeans. She pulled her tank top off over her head and stopped short as she saw herself in the mirror on the bathroom door. Peeking out from the band of her panties just above her crotch was the used condom plastered to her skin. She shook her head to try to clear away the panicky feeling she felt. At least she hadn't found it inside. She tried to recall the details of their intimacy, but it was pretty much a frenzied, fantastic blur.

A different kind of frenzied feeling began later that month when her period failed to arrive.

CHAPTER THREE – "ME AGAIN"

Things for Rachel took off at her work while I was getting closer and closer to the "teacher trap." I had been warned about the mysterious-sounding "teacher trap" time and again by colleagues who loved to complain about what they were doing. "Get out while you can," they would wail loudly at the occasional Friday happy hour. It was the same little group of three or four each time, but they seemed so intense I started to listen more earnestly.

"Oh, god, I should have bolted before I got caught in the teacher trap!" said one disgruntled history teacher.

"I've been in twice as long and I'm gonna be stuck another twenty years past the rest of you. I have six kids and every damn one of them is going to college," moaned another, a health and P.E. teacher who always claimed he couldn't even afford happy hour but somehow always managed to show up.

The gripe session would continue through the shank of the afternoon until everyone paid their tabs and hurried to their cars when they remembered their respective spouses or boyfriends or girlfriends would be impatiently waiting to start their weekends too. No one outside of the teaching profession really felt sorry for anyone in education. The modern educator's life was looked on as some kind of charmed existence with days that ended early and holidays off month after month that collectively surpassed the average working Joe's entire allotment of vacation time for a year. The most annoying perk of all to the world outside was a little thing called "summers off." Admittedly, I always looked at this a bit smugly. If someone wanted to bitch about someone else having every summer off, then maybe he should have considered being a home ec teacher, or putting those math skills to work and teaching calculus. Just don't hate me and the rest of the academic world for having the foresight to realize that having every summer of your life off was worth all the parent/teacher meetings, the in-service days, and all the grading papers put together.

One day in the faculty room I brought up the subject of the "teacher trap" to my best friend at work, the school librarian, June Nicotra.

"What's with the constant carping about some kind of teacher trap from so many teachers at happy hour the other day?" I asked her.

"You did notice, didn't you, that they were all guys, all about the same age? They're all right at about ten years, ready to be tenured in the public education system. Once that happens, you're in the teacher trap," she said.

"I still don't get it. What keeps them trapped? If they want out so badly, why don't they just leave?" I asked, really wanting to know in case it was something vital I should be aware of so I could prevent it from putting me in the same situation.

"Common sense keeps them trapped," she replied

cryptically. It's what I loved about June. Having a conversation with her was fun, like playing a game of twenty questions.

"Explain," I demanded.

"Just around year ten, teachers start to experience what's known in the profession as "burnout.""

She continued despite my effort to interrupt. "Don't worry, you'll get there too. It just so happens that year ten also happens to be the time when you are vested in the retirement system and once you hit that, it's hard to go anywhere without taking a big financial step backwards. So if you listen to what common sense tells you, you stay, and that's what they mean by the "teacher trap." You might as well hunker down because you're going to be doing this for another thirty or forty years. That thought can drive guys your age crazy for some reason."

"So why does being a woman make it any different for you?" I asked.

"That's where the sexes differ. I don't look at it as a trap. I look at it as financial security. Most men never give up on that need to fulfill some kind of childhood dream like being a fireman or a photographer for *National Geographic*. No matter how they look at it, teaching is not exactly a cool, let alone, manly occupation. The burnout factor brings it all to the forefront for them. They start climbing the walls, so to speak."

"When I hear teachers talk about burnout, it really irritates me. I want to tell them to quit whining," I said. "They sound like babies and they give the rest of

45

us a bad name. Every one of my non-teacher friends is already annoyed with me enough every time summer rolls around."

But as time would tell, June was right. Going back to work for my eleventh year in education seemed like a chore. I was losing patience with my English classes and, for the first time, I didn't feel like I was on some kind of crusade to get them to enjoy literature and be better speakers and writers. I felt like I was there to get through the day and get my paycheck and count off the months until summer made its way back onto the calendar.

Rachel noticed how it changed my everyday attitude. I used to pride myself on not using sick days, trying to get my name on the "perfect attendance" list for the year and being among those rewarded with a special dinner at the downtown Hilton, courtesy of the local taxpayers. No wonder the voters got pissed at teachers at contract time. Instead I was finding more and more reasons why I couldn't get out of bed and get myself to work.

I started to adjust my attitude about money too. In the past we had decided that all spare money needed to be hoarded for our children who would someday need cars and weddings and college. After the hysterectomy, that way of thinking was no longer necessary, and gone was the ominous cloud over the bank account we both contributed to. We started vacationing more frequently. It became a hobby and a challenge to finagle more vacation time during the school year without raising any eyebrows or calling attention to the fact that personal days were always getting added on to holidays when possible or sick days turned President's Day into a five day weekend.

Finally Rachel stated what was becoming more and more obvious. "You don't seem to be very happy teaching anymore," she said. "I will totally support your decision if you want to go do something else."

"I can't," I responded, and reminded her that I was in the "teacher trap."

"Well, what about a different position within the school system? You could get certified to be a reading specialist, a special ed teacher, or a principal, or a counselor," she suggested.

"Hmmm," I said. "That's not too bad an idea. Reading specialist is out. I'm irritated enough now as it is by kids who are perfectly capable of reading. Yesterday I had the kids reading Graham Green's *The Third Man* out loud. The book opens by saying 'Harry Lime was penniless,' and the first kid I called on read, 'Harry Lime was penisless.' It would be funny if it wasn't so pathetic. Some of them actually brag about having never read a book."

"And I don't have the patience for special ed. I don't know how those teachers do it. The district doesn't have enough money to pay me to be a principal although they get paid an awful lot to just kiss the superintendent's ass. Counselor. Hmmm. That's worth thinking about. I'm good at solving other people's problems. Kids though, that's a whole different story. I remember a girl in my homeroom crying one time, and I asked her what was wrong. She looked me dead in the eye and told me her boyfriend had dumped her because she wouldn't give him a blow job. Can you imagine saying something like that to a teacher when we were in school? There aren't any limits for kids nowadays."

"You're sounding more and more like your parents," Rachel teased.

Almost ten more years rolled by as I discovered that not thinking about the "teacher trap" was the best way to deal with it. As much as I would have loved to be doing something else, I found it a lot easier to find distraction in a variety of part time jobs. We didn't need the money, but for some reason I was compelled to be out looking for something to fulfill me in the way that teaching used to. The most interesting distraction was playing in a country band. Some friends of mine, very musically inclined, needed a bass player and approached me for the job.

"I can't play the bass, but I want to be in your group. Can't I just sing?" I proposed. I considered my singing voice like a secret weapon that grabbed the limelight at karaoke night or parties that happened to feature someone banging away on a piano. I had strengthened my voice's power and range all my life through ridiculously long practice sessions in the shower or the car.

"Jill is going to do most of the singing," explained her boyfriend Nate. "We want to get hired and we figure featuring a female singer is the best way to draw people in. You'll be fine on the bass because just about every country music song written has maybe four or five chords and you pretty much just alternate notes back and forth." He stuck his brother Phil's bass in my hand and formed my fingers around the neck and onto the frets that matched the chords he was going to play. He started strumming Dolly Parton's "Jolene" and instinctively Phil joined in on banjo. At the same instant I started alternating rhythm notes on the bass. Jill joined in after an appropriate amount of measures as an introduction, and we stumbled through the entire song without stopping. It was an exciting moment when we realized at the same instant that we could actually do this.

Before long, I was living my life around the schedule that Nate dictated for Jill, Phil, and me. We started hitting bars that offered live entertainment to see what we were up against. We did this for several weekends in a row and used the week nights to learn songs. It was completely time consuming, but Rachel didn't seem to mind that suddenly I was never home much. She showed no interest in joining us for the bar hopping or for listening in on the four-hour nightly practice sessions. I assumed she was happy for me, now that I had found a niche that was giving me some kind of renewed purpose. Looking back, I think she was happy being left alone to find her own niche. Every night I would come home to find her either absorbed in reading some huge volume of historical non-fiction or she would be writing page after page in the personal journal she kept. She had filled over a dozen of them, and every Christmas I would hit Borders to buy her a newer, nicer, bigger one.

As a band we were growing impatient to play out. We decided we needed to book a job. This would force us to get our three hours of material completed. We chose a place that had just recently opened, a burger and beer joint near the mall. We figured that a fledgling business would be a good place for a fledgling band to hone its music. After an audition of three songs played with a borrowed PA system, we were hired on the spot. The manager said we could play every weekend from ten P.M. until one in the morning. He would give us three weekends to see how it went and wanted us to start as soon as possible. That was the good news. The bad news was we only had enough material for half of the three hours we would be expected to play. Fortunately, a server stopped at the table we were huddled around and told the manager that there was a phone call for him in the office. It gave us the time we needed to devise a game plan.

"Let me do the talking," said Phil. He had been fairly quiet through rehearsals but now stepped up to take the reins as our business manager. "He's going to want a name to put on the sign outside." It had never occurred to us during all the weeks of rehearsing to come up with a name for the band.

"I've been thinking about that," chimed in Nate. "How about Peanut Brothers and Jilly? Get it? Like peanut butter and jelly....Phil and I are brothers...Jilly...jelly."

Not wanting to insult my friend's suggestion I said, "That's really clever. But don't you think it sounds like a band that someone would hire to play at kids' parties?"

"I agree," said Phil. "It needs to sound more grown up."

"How about The Vienna Boys' Sausage?" Nate suggested. "It's like The Vienna Boys' Choir, mixed with Vienna sausage. People would remember it."

I realized that as talented as Nate was on the guitar and arranging songs, he didn't have much of a knack for naming a band.

Jill chimed in. "It should sound country. If we're playing country music, we need a country sound to the name of the band."

Suddenly the manager reappeared and apologized for the interruption. "All right, let's get this done," he said. "I'd like you to start this Friday."

Phil took over and wowed us with his confidence. "Sorry, no can do. We're booked for the next two weekends already. The earliest we could start is three weekends from now."

"Okay," agreed the manager. "Obviously, you'll be bringing a lot more sound equipment when you actually perform. I thought you'd set up over in that area where you'd be out of the traffic flow from the kitchen."

"Sounds good," said Phil. "We have a few Crate amps, a mix board, and about twice what we have here today for a PA system. That should be just room enough." The three of us stared at Phil in amazement. It was all lies and it was flowing out of him out like shit through a country/western goose.

"I never even asked," said the manager. "What's the name of your band? We have that nice lighted sign outside, and it'll be great to finally have something to put up there."

"Mississippi Mule," declared Phil without missing a beat.

The manager paused for just a second. "Hmmm. That's a lot of letters to get on the sign."

Phil continued, "It's alliterative and it sounds country. And that's our name, take it or leave it." He directed it at the manager, but the three of us were silently nodding in agreement as he spoke.

Every night we would come to practice armed with our own list of favorite songs we thought might work. We'd spend the beginning of each rehearsal by throwing our song ideas out to the group for approval or to be vetoed for some reason. The song pool was huge because Jill's fiddle and Phil's banjo allowed us to broaden our artist list and still give any rendition a country feel. Phil took an occasional lead vocal with Willie Nelson, Kenny Rogers, and Waylon Jennings songs. Jill shone on literally everything she tried and could go from a sweet, quiet Anne Murray tune to a roaring rendition of "Back on the Chain Gang" by The Pretenders. I preferred popular covers from John Denver and "old" Billy Joel and Elton John. Nate went for Crosby, Stills, and Nash, Gene Pitney, and the Beatles.

Our opening was nerve-racking but more fun than I could ever have imagined. We got there hours early, set up the equipment we had borrowed, and then realized we had more than an hour to kill before we had to play. Friends started drifting in to offer their support. Rachel was by herself at a table off to the side. She was eating a salad and reading a book. She would occasionally glance up, tap her watch, and shrug her shoulders as if this would make the evening move faster so she could get home.

At ten minutes to ten, Jill glanced at me and said, "Oh my god, look at you!" I had broken out with a rash that covered every visible inch of my body from head to toe. Even my hands were red and mottled as if I had stuck them under a sun lamp too long. I had never suffered from stage fright before and couldn't understand where this manifestation of nerves was coming from.

We had a successful run of five weeks. The manager was so pleased with the crowds we were drawing that he extended our run from the original three weeks. We huddled together in the bar's kitchen before we began our last night of playing. Jill started tearing up when we talked about the fact that this might be our last night together as a band.

"I wish we could do this forever," she sniffed. "I love you guys."

"Me too," I chimed in. "I was just getting confident on the bass. And look, no rash!" I should have been more careful with what I wished for. As we were loading the band equipment that night we were approached by another local bar owner who proposed booking us for the next four weeks. We jumped at it, especially when he offered us nearly twice the money we had been getting at the burger joint. Here we had thought thirty-five dollars apiece per night was the big time. Rookie mistake.

Eventually I had the feeling I had a foot in each of two traps, the "teacher trap" and now the "band trap." We were playing about forty-five weekends per year, now going into the twelfth year. The venues had gotten bigger but not necessarily better. Bars that demanded a high cover charge drew crowds that felt they had a right to dictate what they wanted to hear. Bars that asked for no cover charge were jammed with hordes of people drunk on quarter drafts who wanted to hear "Rocky Top" at least once every half hour. I finally had enough when a particularly obnoxious drunk asked if he could sing "Happy Birthday" on the microphone for his friend's thirtieth birthday. By that time we were adept at reading drunks. This idiot was not going away. The only thing to do was to let him get it over with quickly.

It was more embarrassing than usual. He swayed back and forth and began with a heartfelt belch that ripped through the speakers. "Chuck. Buddy. This is for you, you fucking asshole." He began singing "Happy Birthday" at the top of his lungs. We began playing along with him while he sang. There was a reason for this; it gave us some element of control over the tempo so we could move him along and be done. Unfortunately it also tied us to instruments, making any attempt at self-defense impossible. Just as Rock Star got to the clever ending, "Happy birthday, you douche bag, happy birth…" it rained garbage.

Chuck, the birthday boy, thought it would be really fun to make a critical commentary on his friend's singing. He picked up a huge trash barrel sitting next to the bar. It was filled with wet popcorn, dirty paper plates, and just about anything nasty someone felt like throwing into the barrel that particular evening. Chuck was a hulking guy who obviously worked out regularly just for occasions like this. He hoisted the dripping barrel over his head with one hand on the handle and the other hand supporting the bottom. He took a mad swing and shot the contents of the barrel from about ten paces. The trash managed to pretty much cover each of us and every piece of band equipment we owned. Nate and Phil whipped off their instruments, set them in their stands, and immediately shoved the guest singer off the stage who commenced to pounding Chuck with his fists. A brawl was breaking out in front of me, but all I could see was the look of shock and embarrassment on Jill's face as she stood there. Her right arm was extended, holding on to her precious fiddle which was dripping with something that looked like ranch dip and cigarette butts.

She and I quietly began wiping down the equipment with some bar rags that were sitting on a nearby stool. After the bouncer and a few of Rock Star and Chuck's friends got things settled down, Nate and Phil came back to check on us.

"This sucks," said Nate. "But Chuck has a conscience at least. He felt bad about throwing shit at us and told us to split this." He extended two fifty dollar bills. It made no impact on me, nor did it remove the angry look that had taken over Jill's face.

"I told him, for another hundred he could pee on us next time," said Phil, trying to lighten the mood.

Driving home I decided that getting covered in garbage was not worth twenty-five extra dollars. If I had to sing "Good Timin' Woman" one more time I was going to have to hurt someone. If one more old lady at a wedding reception yelled that we were too loud, I was going to lose it. We had an unusual lull in bookings coming up, and it was the right time to bow out.

The void I created for myself by leaving the band had to be filled. I thought Rachel and I would finally have time to do things, but after twelve years of being a band widow, she seemed fairly uninterested in any of my suggestions for how we might spend my new-found spare time.

I had never paid much attention to personal physical fitness, but years of free band drinks and bar food had put enough extra pounds on me that it made sense to make exercise my next distraction. The two standard lines I had started spouting jokingly to laugh off the extra weight weren't sounding so funny after a year of saying them. The first: I'm fighting the battle against anorexia...and winning. The second: Six pack abs? I can beat that. I have a quarter keg.

In six months time with walking, tennis, racquetball, and Weight Watchers, I was down to the trimmest I had been since high school. My new found fitness deserved some reward. Of all things, I found going to bars to be fun again. I had spent so many years working in them and not being able to relax. Suddenly going out didn't mean working anymore; it meant letting loose and having fun. I was even more driven to be out on the town when summer rolled around. I had fallen in with a couple of different barfly gangs that kept track of the days of the week by Trivia Night, Dollar Import Night, Karaoke Night, Open Mike Night, and a stream of other gimmicks that promised a good time.

I had lost the desire to be in a band, I had lost close to forty pounds, and somewhere along the way, I lost Rachel. She made the observation one day that we didn't really have that much in common anymore. She wanted to know what I thought of moving to another state. She was tired of living in the same place her whole life. A few months earlier her mother had passed away, and her father had passed just about a year before that.

"I really can't go," I told her.

"Why not?" she wondered.

"The "teacher trap." If I hang in there just a little while longer, I'm good to go," I explained.

It turned out she was good to go right then. And so she went. It was quick and fairly amicable. There were moments of incredible sadness but, feeling like we had no other choice, we just worked through those. Somehow we knew we were doing what needed to be done.

Our friends were surprised. They commiserated separately with each of us. I imagine they told the two of us what they thought we might want to hear. Without fail, everyone eventually got around to emphasizing one point. At least we didn't have to worry about dealing with kids while divorcing. I guess it did make it easier without kids in the picture. Once again, I viewed my life as something that was all mine, uncomplicated by a child. I hadn't yet met Jamie Jernigan. But I would soon.

CHAPTER FOUR – "JAMIE AGAIN"

It's not like Jamie had completely sworn off men. She had just sworn off sleeping with them. What really irritated her was that she immensely enjoyed sex both times she had had it, and she found herself thinking about it a lot. After her home pregnancy test confirmed what she already knew to be true, she wondered if she was being punished for some reason. Certainly not just for having sex. Everyone she knew had sex, and they weren't always given a door prize each time that required feeding and changing and doctor bills and clothes to grow out of. In order to not drive herself crazy, she convinced herself that having two babies was not a punishment. Her boys were rewards. She must have done something really wonderful to have gone two for two in the conception department. And she loved her boys. As soon as Little Vincent was old enough, she was back in the academic world, this time dropping both her boys at the day care provided by Edinboro University. It was a program identical to the one that Slippery Rock had offered.

After Vincent was born the decision to change schools had been easy. Before she left Slippery Rock, she sat in her English Literature class one day listening to a quirky English professor named Tristan Welch leading a discussion of Sherwood Anderson's *Winesburg, Ohio*. He seemed obsessed with a female character of questionable morals that he enjoyed describing as the "town pump." He strode across the room and parked himself on the edge of her desk as he asked the class their feelings about the role this woman played in the novel. Jamie was pretty sure no one knew of her pregnant condition, yet she couldn't conceal the fact that her face was flushing red. It was a safe bet that Bill wouldn't have told anyone that she was carrying his baby. His way of dealing with impending fatherhood was much different than Darrell's had been. He disappeared. He was still on campus, but he was completely gone from Jamie's life. She had offered Bill the same opportunity as Darrell that would allow him to opt out of any responsibility. He offered her an apology but nothing else, not even a tin ring. Not that she would have accepted it. If nothing else she was determined to learn from her mistakes. She decided it made sense to finish the first semester and work full time to save money so that she could afford to go right back to school after baby number two was born. Darrell was a huge help, taking both boys when she needed him to. There was never any hint of judgment on his part when they communicated, and for that she was grateful.

She had named Vincent after Vincent Van Gogh. The artist was her favorite, his style and fearless use of color was something she loved on an emotional level and felt she understood on an artistic level. Her other favorite was Jackson Pollock. She would often paint with the *Pollock* DVD playing as background.

She pretty much knew the entire movie by heart. She didn't know if Ed Harris had won any awards for his portrayal of the tortured artist, but she sure would have given him the Oscar without a second thought. So Vincent was almost named Jackson. It had been a close contest, but when she first saw him she said, "Hello, Little Vincent," without even thinking about it, and that was it.

Jamie fell into a very contented existence with her painting and her two boys. The bar she waitressed in on weekend nights was a godsend. It catered more to the faculty crowd, and it was rare to see any of the students mingling in with them. Drinks were expensive, and the menu was equally pricey. This kept the financially strapped co-eds away. Obviously the professors and college administrators didn't mind paying higher prices for the peace and quiet and privacy it gave them. High prices meant high tips and allowed Jamie to maintain her balancing act while going to school. Every time money did become an issue, there seemed to be some windfall out of the blue that saved her, if only temporarily. She found it very satisfying when these little moments of good fortune came from her painting. She had been commissioned to paint a mural on the outside wall of a pet store in town. It was a feel-good menagerie of every kind of pet sold in the store, and people just seemed to smile when they saw it. Word spread in the small college town that the artist was local, a student at the college. About once a month another business would call her to design and execute a painting on a wall in a waiting room, or an inviting sign over a store's entrance. She became known for creating interesting logos that combined the names of the businesses with colorful images that people would remember and recognize later.

She had learned to live without much sleep, not that she had much of a choice. Some days she would drop the boys off at campus day care, attend her classes, pick them up, feed them, bathe them, play a game or paint with them, and reluctantly put them to bed. Trisha, her next door neighbor, usually knocked on her door around eight-thirty every weeknight. It was another of those little miracles that seemed to drop out of nowhere. Trisha loved to baby sit and would have done it gladly without pay. She loved getting out of the house and away from her nagging mother who was constantly on her back about everything. Jamie insisted on paying her, but Trisha said from the start that she'd do it for a dollar an hour and whatever food she might scrounge from the refrigerator. She didn't want to jeopardize the good thing she had going with the refuge right next door. Even on nights that Jamie didn't need her for babysitting, Trisha would often find an excuse to hang out. She would drift to the kitchen to talk on the phone with her boyfriend and then join Jamie in the cramped living room to watch television while Jamie painted at the second-hand drafting table she had purchased at a garage sale. Jamie enjoyed the company, even if it was just a teenaged girl who talked incessantly about rock bands Jamie had never heard of. This happy arrangement continued for two years until Trisha graduated from high school and eventually escaped from her mother's house by enrolling at Pitt to study business. Jamie soon discovered how much she missed her neighbor's babysitting and her friendship. There were a couple of backup babysitters in the area, but they were going to put a bigger strain on Jamie's funds. She could manage for one more year until she would graduate with an art degree and a teaching certificate. Again she lucked out by getting a student teaching assignment at the local high school, less than a three mile drive from campus and her apartment.

Jamie was pinch-bartending one evening when one of her favorite art teachers, Amy Eisert, walked in and took a corner stool at the bar. "Good evening, Dr. Eisert. What can I get for you?" Jamie asked as she grabbed a rag and cleaned the area in front of the professor. The bar was already spotless, but she wanted to make a good impression.

"I'll have a gin and tonic, thanks," replied Dr. Eisert. "I was going to speak to you after class tomorrow, but there's something I'd like to run past you right now if you have a moment."

Fortunately the bar was slow, allowing Jamie the chance for some uninterrupted chat time with her instructor. "Sure. What's it about?"

Dr. Eisert waited until Jamie placed her drink in front of her and continued. "First of all, how's student teaching going? It must be a lot to handle. I remember you telling me in class that you have two boys at home."

"It's going fine. Sometimes there aren't enough hours in the day, but I can see the light at the end of the tunnel," replied Jamie.

"Well, that's precisely what I wanted to talk to you about. When you reach the end of that tunnel, do you have any immediate plans?"

"Sure. I have to find a job as soon as possible. I'm already mapping out school districts I want to apply to for a teaching job. Why do you ask?" Jamie shook a bag of Chex Mix into a bowl and set it in front of Dr. Eisert.

"I think you have real potential as a commercial artist. It just so happens I have a friend in business who is looking for an intern in commercial design. It doesn't pay a lot, but it's a tremendous opportunity for someone starting out. I can't think of any of my students who would be better suited for it than you," said Dr. Eisert.

"I'm really flattered. Wow! I can't believe this." Jamie's pulse raced with the thought of being out in the real world and being able to work in her field.

Dr. Eisert continued. "There are some details that you would have to consider, mostly demographic. It's an advertising agency in New Jersey. It would involve uprooting your life here to move there, but it's a very successful, respected company. Depending on your performance, it could possibly lead to something in the way of a career using your art degree. I have to admit, I wonder sometimes how some of the students here are actually going to make a living as an artist when they get out of here. You, I think, have what it takes."

"I'll do it. That is, if you wouldn't mind telling whoever it is that I'm interested," Jamie said excitedly.

"There's some time to think it over. I know you'll want to consider what the offer really consists of before you make a commitment. It's in Newark, certainly a much bigger city than you're used to. If the higher cost of living and the relocation isn't an issue, I'd love to see you go for it. I'll tell my friend you're interested and have him contact you for an interview. Again, I'm not sure what it pays, but I think he said their internships generally last for at least six months." Dr. Eisert pushed her empty glass forward and stood up.

"I really appreciate this. I wouldn't let you down," said Jamie.

"I have no doubt," replied Dr. Eisert as she made her way to join some other faculty members who were seated at a nearby table.

The rest of Jamie's shift was a blur as she imagined her life moving in a new direction, one that she hadn't even considered before. She had never thought of doing anything other than teaching. Wasn't this an even better opportunity? She had wanted out of Titusville even when she was younger, ever since movies and television had shown her what life could be in a big city. Now here she was on the brink of moving to the east coast for a chance to make her mark as an artist.

She and Dr. Eisert submitted photos of her work. Not only did Jamie need the approval of her teacher's friend, there were others within the company who had a say. A glowing recommendation from an art professor was one thing, but the powers that be needed to see what she was capable of before they would make a decision.

A week later her prayers were answered. After a phone interview and an offer on the table, the decision was up to her. She had taken the call in Dr. Eisert's office so that a proper introduction could be made. She thanked her professor and headed home on top of the world but at the same time, under a dark cloud. She had spoken to Darrell about this big break lurking on the horizon. They discussed the practicality of her being able to afford to live in a bigger city, paying rent, paying for sitters, and managing her living expenses. It would have to have been a generous offer, and the odds of an internship offering much more than a meager stipend were not very good. She had prepared herself for the worst, and she wasn't let down. At best she would be able to survive by herself, but there was no way on earth she would be able to have the boys with her. She kept telling herself that she was doing this for them. It was the best option she had for giving them a decent life, even if it meant some sacrifice. Darrell had agreed that if the terms were not up to what she hoped for, he would manage somehow to take the boys for the six month term.

Jamie threw her keys on the coffee table, paid the babysitter, and immediately went to the bedroom that

Darrell and Vincent shared. As usual, they were waiting for her to come in and say goodnight and sat up in their beds as soon as she slowly opened their door to peek in.

"So did you get the job, Mom?" Darrell asked.

"It's not really a job, Honey. It's a place where I'd go to learn more about how to do the work I want to do," she replied.

"You don't need to do that," Darrell said. "You're the best painter in the world right now."

"Didn't your teacher tell them that?" added Vincent.

It never ceased to amaze Jamie how much of her life her kids picked up on. She never remembered speaking directly to them about the internship, but they must have heard her on the phone with her ex husband.

"Well, they want me to come work with them, but I have a week to think about it before I decide," she said. Then Jamie started the nightly ritual that had grown out of both boys' fascination with airplanes and airports. She kissed her hand and blew the kiss up toward the ceiling light in the center of the room. A second later she repeated the act a second time.

The two boys started darting their eyes around the ceiling of the room. Vincent, the more impatient of the two, jumped up and fell back down on the bed waving his arms at the ceiling. "Here it comes. It's circling. It's approaching the runway. It's about to land!" He grabbed at the air and then smacked himself lightly on the face. "And it's on the ground, safe and sound."

Little Darrell waited until his brother finished his half of the game before he started yelling to the ceiling. "Here it comes. It's hovering over LAX. It's gone! It's already approaching O'Hare. Oh no! It doesn't have enough gas to reach JFK. Yes it does! Here it comes! And it's right on time." He reached above him grabbing the imaginary plane and pulled his hand back down as Vincent had done, tapping his face with his open palm. "On the ground, safe and sound!" The boys laughed and kicked their feet as they crawled under the covers.

"I love you," she called to them as she turned off the light and closed their door. She didn't need a week to make her decision. There was no way she was leaving them.

CHAPTER FIVE – "ME AND JAMIE"

My head was pounding just loud enough, I thought maybe I had overslept and someone was knocking on my bedroom door to wake me up in time for work. That didn't make any sense. There hadn't been anyone in months who would have performed such a polite service for me. Rachel had been gone since May and it was already mid-July. Her last wifely duty was to get me to the family doctor who readily prescribed the popular antidepressant of the month. Rachel had diagnosed me with depression over her pending departure, and I never admitted it out loud, but she was right. I had taken to coming home from work and drinking wine while sitting on the floor near the fireplace and blowing cigarette smoke up the fireplace chimney. Eventually I developed the habit of taking my antidepressant after dinner and then going out drinking just about every night of the week. I didn't feel as depressed, but I wasn't sure whether it was the Cymbalta or the booze that was making the difference.

Before seeing the doctor I had called my old friend Brett to find out what drug he was currently on. He updated me frequently on his latest find. He went from Zoloft to Xanex and eventually to Cymbalta. Plus Brett could be a sympathetic ear, albeit a long-distance one. He had moved to Pittsburgh a couple of years earlier to take a job near where his wife was from. He had tried selling used cars in Erie, but he was just too nice and too honest to make a go of it. His used car-selling brother Matt had talked him into joining him at the car lot. Matt had sold Brett a car a month earlier. It was a piece of crap, but Brett marveled at how smoothly Matt had convinced him that it was the only car he could "see him in." Matt, as they say, could sell ice to an Eskimo. Brett couldn't sell a blanket to one.

Brett had gone through the divorce thing and therefore seemed to me to be somewhat of an authority on survival advice. His story was much more dramatic than mine. His wife had left him abruptly and had taken their baby and moved in with her new boyfriend. Word filtered back home and our entire old circle of friends who knew them before their move was shocked at her uncharacteristic behavior. We didn't know the half of it. One night Brett called and invited me down for a visit. I met him at an Olive Garden right off the thruway.

"So you've joined the club," he said as a way of greeting me. He got out of the booth and gave me a sympathetic hug. I barely got to say a word as he unloaded his story on me. It was distracting, not to mention fascinating, but I felt I had been mislead. I thought this was supposed to be about me and my more-recent-than-his divorce.

"No matter what you're going through, it can't compare to what I've been through in the past year," he said.

"Well, you got a beautiful kid out of the deal. And

I'm glad you followed in my footsteps and joined a band. You'll meet lots of new people that way," I offered. Brett and I shared the same passion for singing, and he had filled the position as lead singer for a rock band.

"And look at you," I said. "You don't have an ounce of fat on you, and you're dressed like a rock star."

"It's part of my bounce back therapy. My parents came down to hear the band. I was so excited for them to see what I'm doing now, and all my mom could talk about was how skinny I am. I told her I looked that way because I had lost 120 pounds of bitch!" Brett flagged the waitress down for more drinks.

"So what's the problem?" I asked.

"The kid's not mine."

"What?"

"You heard me. I love him. I claimed him on the birth certificate as my own. But I'm not the biological father."

"How do you know? Did she tell you that? And why would she fess up to that?" This was like something out of *The National Enquirer*, and I was all ears.

"She didn't have a choice," Brett continued. "There was no way it could have been mine because we hadn't done it for almost six months. It was when I started experimenting with the antidepressants and the Cymbalta had pretty much shut down my equipment. By the way, don't go on the Cymbalta."

I made the mental note to never take the Cymbalta

again.

I left Pittsburgh admiring how Brett had faced his circumstances head on and moved forward. His advice to me was well intended, but amounted to nothing more than common sense that any self-help book might have to offer: pick yourself up and move on. He knew from previous long talks that having a child wasn't a priority of mine, but pointed out that we were getting "up there" in age and if I was going to be a father, I'd better get on the ball and find someone who wanted to be a mother.

I met Jamie that fall. I heard that the school had hired a new art teacher, and she was already the talk of the men's faculty. Most of them referred to her as the hot new blonde in the art room. This also made her the talk of the female faculty members, sharing their disapproval of Jamie's tendency to dress like one of the students and being a little too friendly with the male teachers who shared the same hallway as the art room. When she walked into the first faculty meeting of the new school year, heads turned. She was a little loud, her hair a little too wild, and she glanced around the library to find a seat. It was very noticeable that a number of the men tried nonchalantly to indicate an empty seat conveniently unoccupied next to them. She chose, completely at random I believe, a seat directly across the room from me. She sat down at a reading table and unloaded the armful of art supplies she had just picked up from the supply room. During the meeting, I noticed she pretended to be paying attention to the agenda while constantly drawing on the legal pad in front of her. When the time arrived on the meeting's agenda for the principal to introduce the new faculty members, she put her pencil down and waited her turn. When her name was called she stood and addressed the room.

"Hi. I'm Jamie Jernigan. I'm originally from Titusville. I recently finished my art education degree from Edinboro University, and this is my first teaching job. I'm a single mother with two kids. My younger one is out of high school as of last June, and I decided it would be a good time for me to relocate. I taught some middle school art for a while, but my first choice was always to get a high school art position. And I would totally appreciate any help or suggestions anyone has since I'm brand new to teaching this age group." She flashed a smile to the entire room as she sat down. The men were all smiling back as they nodded up and down. Most of the women were pursing their lips while their heads moved side to side.

I rarely had the opportunity to see Jamie. I was two floors above her, and our paths never seemed to cross except for the occasional time when we'd pass each other in the mail room or at the Xerox machine in the main office.

It wasn't until months later that I even spoke to her. I was leaving the Plymouth Tavern after a Friday night of drinks with some neighbors. As I passed her table she grabbed the sleeve of my sweater and pulled me into the booth to sit next to her. She introduced me to her table of drinking buddies as the only member of the faculty she hadn't met yet.

In the few minutes I sat with her I noticed two things. One, she dominated but did not monopolize the conversation. She was like Julie from *The Love Boat*, who took charge of organizing everyone's fun. Two, the four guys at the table rarely took their eyes off of her. The only other person she bothered to introduce to me by name was the only other female at the table. It was her best friend Lorene who had also recently moved to Erie after getting married to her high school sweetheart. She was model-beautiful and worked at JCPenney.

For some reason I felt intimidated by this group. The two girls were a few years younger than I was, and the guys were a couple of decades younger than I was. I later found out that Jamie and Lorene had just met them that evening on their girls' night out.

I made an excuse to leave, but Jamie pulled me back down next to her and slapped my leg with surprising force. "You're not going anywhere," she said. "I'm buying you a drink."

That drink was followed by a few more as we politely kept taking turns getting the next one. The more she talked to me, the more the other guys turned their attention to Lorene. In the hour that followed, I saw an entirely different girl emerge from behind the outgoing persona that seemed to take over whatever room she was in. Somehow I knew she was out to have some fun, but I sensed she had no interest in hooking up with any of the other guys at the table. As we shared our back stories with each other, I increasingly felt there was an innocence and sweetness to her. It pulled on me like a magnet. As she told me about her struggle with kids and colleges and parents and boyfriends, I also sensed sadness and insecurity that I figured not many others were privy to. Suddenly out of the blue I found myself offering her an invitation.

"A friend of mine from high school, Gary, and his partner want me to find someone to take swing dance lessons with at the community center," I blurted out. "It's Tuesday nights for six weeks, and it's only forty bucks."

"Oh, my God, that sounds like fun. Sign us up. Who are we doing this with?" she asked.

"My friend Gary. The band I was in played his wedding years ago, but now he's one of the many divorced friends I've found myself hanging out with. He decided to go a new route, so to speak, and he has a boyfriend now. They're really great. You'll love them."

"I'm sure I will. Hey, if Lorene didn't just get married to Super Stud, I was about ready to hook up with her!" she laughed. The other side of the table got noticeably quiet for just a second. "I'm kidding, morons," she said, relieving their anxiety about having wasted their beer money on a pair of attractive lesbians.

"How long have you been divorced?" I asked.

"Quite a while," Jamie responded casually. "Two different dads for two different kids. I was married to the first one. That's just the way it is."

"Well, then that's the way it should be," I assured her. I thought it sounded like a stupid thing to say and didn't expect the reaction I got.

"That's what I keep telling myself," she said. "I love that we think alike. And I'm glad you stopped by to say hi finally."

"That's not exactly the way it went down," I reminded her. "But I know what you mean."

"Stop by downstairs Monday morning for coffee. I make it right in my room, but I'd bring your own mug if I were you. I think my room is at the top of the list of the rooms they forget to clean at night," she said.

On Monday morning I got to work early, and with coffee mug in hand I went down to Jamie's room. She was sitting in her little office with her feet up, already drinking coffee.

She immediately fired a question at me. "Did I actually agree to take swing lessons with you, or did I just dream that? Because I don't dance."

"You agreed to it. You actually seemed excited about it, as a matter of fact," I said.

"Oh, my God, how much had I been drinking?"

"Obviously enough to agree to take swing dance lessons."

"And I take it you would be offended if I backed out?"

"Offended? Not really. Hurt? Yes."

"Oh, you're good at this," she said, smacking me on the arm with the ruler from her desk. "Alright, I'll do it, just as long as we're clear on one thing. I'll do the swing thing, but then you owe me one. But it's gonna be big, and it's gonna be my choice."

"Deal," I said. "And I want to thank you for listening to me drone on about my sorry, single life. It felt good to talk to somebody new."

"I think you're going to be okay," Jamie said smiling. "And me too. And, by the way, I hope you keep the things I told you about me to yourself. I'm the new girl here, and I don't need the world to know everything about me."

"Not to worry," I replied. "I hardly talk to anybody here,"

But in less than a year, that's exactly what would happen. The whole country would know her story. And mine.

CHAPTER SIX – "POOL PARTY"

I have always sought organization and structure. Maybe that's why I was drawn to teaching in the first place. Keeping a flawless grade book gave me a sense of pride and fulfillment. I kept a calendar on the refrigerator, one on my desk at work, one behind my desk at work, and during the school year I carried one of those fold-over pocket calendars almost everywhere I went. When I had time to myself I enjoyed a strange ritual. On whatever calendar was closest at hand, I would fill in any event, meeting, obligation, upcoming vacation, or birthday that I needed to remember. Then I would flip back month by month, taking a trip through the things that were past. Then I would flip ahead and try to commit to memory all of the things to look forward to. Not that I considered my preoccupation with calendars obsessive, but when Rachel and I were married, she stopped adding anything on the refrigerator calendar when she saw how her intrusion into my calendar territory made me edgy. She never called me on it, though now I'm sure she might have plenty to say about some of my unusual habits. Another one was alphabetizing CD's and DVD's…by category.

This might explain the one problem I always experienced with having the summer off every year. I suddenly was without the regular routine of work. At first I relished every day of sleeping in and having the time to do nothing, but by mid-summer I found myself antsy and searching for something to give my days structure. The summer after my first year of working with Jamie, all of that changed. On the very first day of summer vacation she called me early in the morning to announce that today was Pool Party. She lived in an apartment complex just a short drive or bike ride away from where I lived. Residents were allowed up to four guests at the pool at any given time. When she moved in, she quickly introduced herself to her neighbors and assessed their willingness to cooperate with her Pool Party plan. The ones that were friendly never blinked an eye when she asked if she could sign friends in under their names if she needed some extra spots.

I arrived at the first Pool Party of the summer very unprepared. Jamie was seated in the middle of a blanket on the cement pool deck. On a nearby patio table sat a huge glass jar with a spigot. I would soon become familiar with the "drink of the day" concept, usually a flavored vodka mixed with either iced tea or lemonade.

"Get a drink and get over here!" Jamie shouted as I pulled my car into a spot near the chain link pool fencing. I hadn't even gotten out of the car yet. It seemed as if she was holding court with some neighbor ladies, her daughter-in-law to be, and a few good-looking tanned guys who were constantly jockeying to get their beach towels in a closer proximity to hers. Through quick introductions I learned that four out of five of the men were divorced or separated, a common link with many of the residents of this apartment complex. On the days they had their turn with their kids, the pool was a cheap way of entertaining them. The lifeguard served as a free babysitter for kids of all ages who never seemed to want to get out of the pool. Other teachers, some from our school district and some from neighboring districts, were the mainstays that were there every day. And I mean every day. From about ten in the morning until four in the afternoon Pool Party became a way of life for the entire summer. All participants groaned a little every day when Jamie would start packing up the red wagon that had once belonged to Little Darrell. Now it was a transport for Jamie's towels, blanket, water bottles, backgammon board, magazines, and suntan lotion. The last item packed safely in among the towels was the glass jug, and it was always empty.

After a few days of polite socializing, and once everyone got to know one another, the tournaments started. The "regulars" patiently waited their turns as backgammon, gin rummy, and Yahtzee games were being played at different tables or blankets around the area of the pool we had claimed. Suddenly I had a new routine, and I loved it. No more was there a need to do anything at home but make the bed and head out the door. A stop at the Country Fair took care of all the day's necessities: snacks to throw onto the community snack pile, cold drinks on the days when I couldn't face "drink of the day" that early, a combo sub meal-deal, and two scratch-off lottery tickets. The first time I had shown up with lottery tickets, it had been a spur of the moment purchase. Jamie was so excited during the scratching process, I got a kick out of it. I started bringing them everyday and would wait until she would say something like, "Hey! When are you going to scratch those so we can be millionaires?" before making a big production of getting a coin out of my knapsack to check them. Secretly I enjoyed it whenever she referred to things in terms of "we." I felt this way despite the fact that I knew I was nothing even close to her "type." I was eight years older than she was, and she seemed to enjoy flirting with guys who were at least double our age difference younger. We'd been out together enough for me to see what she was drawn to, mostly the tall, more rugged, type A guys that I had long given up trying to emulate. It never bothered me because at the end of the evening when our favorite haunts were closing down, she would either get in my car for a ride home or ask me to follow her home on the evenings we had driven separately. I'm sure these guys, nameless beer guzzlers who were attracted to her, wondered who this older guy was that she always eventually found her way back to. I'm not surprised because I wondered that myself. I never questioned her about it. I didn't want to press my luck. I had never felt a stronger bond of friendship with anyone. The thought of kissing her had crossed my mind, but I realized that more than anything, to Jamie I was some kind of safety net. I guess women seldom think of kissing their safety nets.

One day I pulled into my spot outside the pool fence and didn't get the usual wave from Jamie. She was in the middle of an obviously intense game of gin rummy with a guy I had never seen at Pool Party before. His back was to me, and all I could see was that he was very tan and built like a brick shithouse. I approached their table and plunked my knapsack and plastic Country Fair bags onto the table.

Without ever moving her eyes from the discard pile, Jamie introduced me to someone she referred to as one of her best friends, Anson. You would think as her best friend, I would have known all of her other best friends by now. In the middle of her introduction she interrupted herself with a resounding, "Fuck you, buddy!" as Anson turned his discard upside down on the pile and splayed his gin hand with a smart-ass flourish.

"Alright, that puts you at two and a half cases you owe me," were the first words I had ever heard Anson speak. Jamie's favorite bet for her poolside gambling habit was a half-case of beer. I honestly believed for weeks that someone actually was keeping track of who owed what to whom, until I realized that there was never a payoff time. Every once in a while someone would show up with a fancier-than-usual drink of the day and declare that he was even with everyone at the pool that he owed half-cases of beer. These occasional declarations were always met with agreeable head-nodding and shouts of "Cool!" or "Right on, buddy!" from whoever happened to be at

Pool Party that day. It was a fun, friendly, fantastic way to spend the summer.

Anson glanced at me. "Sit down, partner," he said. "You're my next victim. How about a half-case of winner's choice?"

"Okay," I agreed. I would have preferred playing for some Bacardi, but it didn't matter since no one ever paid up their debts.

Anson lit a little grape flavored cigar and dealt the cards. Jamie watched from her patio chair and razzed Anson each time I'd calmly lay down my cards and declare gin. We alternated wins for a while until I hit a streak and won a few in a row. Jamie got quieter and appeared nervous, as if I would be committing some social indiscretion by beating this self-assured guy on my first time out.

I was a little put off when I realized it wasn't my imagination that she was rooting for him. "Come on, Anson. If you can beat me, you can certainly beat him!" she shouted.

"Hey, I beat you plenty of times. What's the deal here? I don't exactly suck at gin," I said in my own defense.

Two hands later I achieved victory.

"Wow! Unbelievable!" Jamie declared. Was it really so inconceivable that I had won? That's when I realized that Jamie really liked this guy.

"What'll it be, champ?" Anson asked.

"Bud Light Lime," I responded.

Suddenly Jamie was back to tease mode. "Anson, I can't believe he took you on his first time." She laughed and gave him the punch in the arm that was usually reserved for me.

"Ahh, I took it easy on him," said Anson.

"Oh, sure. And why did you do that?" she asked.

"I just met him. It's called being polite."

I knew he was kidding. But I also saw he was rationalizing the loss at the same time. I thought he was pretty cool.

I eventually learned a lot about my new friend. He taught middle school math in the city and coached football. He usually had to cut out early every day to get to practice. He joined Pool Party a few weeks late because he had been taking a three-week grad class toward his Master's in special ed. He had a girlfriend named Kelly who worked for GE, and they had recently been out to dinner for the second anniversary of their first date. I had trouble processing this in light of the fact that it was obvious that Anson had "a thing" for Jamie and I was pretty sure the feeling was mutual on her part.

Anson had officially become part of the gang, and I was disappointed one day to discover he was not in his usual chair when I pulled in next to the fence.

"Where's Anson?" I tossed the question directly to Jamie.

"He has football camp for the next two weeks," she responded. "He'll be back after that."

It was kind of nice to once again have more of her attention, but Anson's absence created a noticeable void for a few days until we got used to him not being there lighting up his little cigars, fiddling with his iPod and dealing cards.

"So what's the story with you and Anson?" I asked Jamie out of the blue during a lull in conversation.

She handed me a bottle of suntan lotion and turned to face away from me. I started applying Maui Babe on her shoulders and back as she told the story of their brief history. She met him in a bar one night and took his challenge for a game of pool. He was on a temporary breakup from Kelly, and she could tell from his cautious behavior that he was probably counting on getting back with the ex-girlfriend he occasionally referenced. The platonic courtship went on for a couple of weeks, and during that time they started to realize how much they enjoyed spending time together.

"How is it I never heard a word about this guy before?" I asked.

"You were at your brother's in Minnesota when this all happened," Jamie replied.

"So how serious do you see yourself with him?"

"I have to tell you, I really like him. But he's back with Kelly now, and there are other factors that enter into this."

Now it was getting interesting, and in her usual way she drew me into the story. "Go on," I said.

"Well, we made out a couple of times. Drinking was involved. But it's more than just the fooling around. We really have a great time together. You know how sometimes people just click? I'm a champ at keeping my guard up, but I have to tell you, I was really starting to fall for him. No one else knows this, but he told me to say the word and he was ready to end it with Kelly."

"So what's the problem? I can tell that you're really into each other."

"He's twelve years younger," she began.

"Like that's ever stopped you before!" I interrupted.

"But that's not the deal breaker," she continued, ignoring my teasing. "He wants to get married and start a family. I'm so far past that. You of all people know my position on that. So that's that."

"You're still young enough to pop another one out," I said. "Maybe one would be enough for him. You really can't see yourself going through motherhood one more time? I mean, if you think he's the one, maybe you should just bite the bullet and go for it."

"Let me clear this up once and for all. I have no problem with having another baby. I just don't want to raise another baby. I love my two boys more than anything in the world, but I'm done. I don't even consider it an option."

"How does he feel about Darrell and Vincent? I mean, he'd be an instant dad."

"Not enough, I guess. He wants his own, and I can understand that. Too bad, though."

"What do you mean?"

"I love the idea of going through the whole baby thing. Despite the circumstances I was in each time before, I really loved being pregnant. I just can't sign

E-baby

on for another kid, just when I'm getting these two out of the house. In case you haven't noticed, I enjoy my freedom. It was hard raising two kids, basically on my own. Don't get me wrong. Looking back I honestly wouldn't change a thing. I actually got into the T-ball thing, little league, and karate. My boys were my life, and the past fourteen or fifteen years since I decided to stay put in this area have flown by. But now that they're old enough, I'm ready to get back to concentrating on what the next best thing for me should be."

"Okay. How about this? Reel Anson in, enjoy your nine months of impending motherhood, and maybe you'll feel differently. If you're still not up to the task of raising it, just sell it on eBay."

"Sell what on eBay?" Lorene said as she threw a blanket down next to us and began unwrapping her burrito from Taco Bell. Lorene was an eBay fanatic. Buying junk at garage sales and selling it on eBay was her second occupation, and her interest in our conversation was genuine.

"Jamie wants to have another baby, but she doesn't necessarily want to keep it. So I told her to sell it on eBay." Lorene is the only person I know who would not have realized immediately that I was joking.

"Can you do that? That's terrible. Who would ever think of selling a baby?" she asked, quite seriously.

Jamie joined in the fun. "Yes, we were just discussing how there are so many couples that can't

87

have kids, and how nice it would be if we made a baby for someone who wasn't able to. I really think we might do it."

Suddenly I was going to be a dad. I figured for some reason, Jamie didn't want Lorene to know that Anson was the true intended father of her next child. Lorene looked at me like I was crazy to go along with such a ridiculous idea. "I think it's illegal," she said.

"I'm pretty sure two consenting adults having a baby, even out of wedlock, is not illegal," I responded.

"No, idiot. Selling it would be illegal. I'm pretty sure you'd get arrested if you tried to sell a baby on eBay."

"Nonetheless, we're considering it," I said. "I think Jamie and I would produce a beautiful child." I wanted to laugh, but I wasn't sure if Jamie was through playing with Lorene's head.

Lorene stood up from her blanket. "You're both insane," she said. "I need a Pepsi. Do either of you want anything from the machines?" she asked as she grabbed her beach bag and dug for some change.

"No, I'm good. Jamie, do you want anything?" I looked at Jamie who was staring at the kids splashing around in the pool. She looked deep in thought and didn't respond. "I guess not," I answered for her. Lorene shrugged her shoulders and started off across the hot cement on her quest for something cold to drink.

"What," I said to Jamie, not really making it a question.

"Let's do it," she said, never taking her eyes off the pool.

"Let's do what?" I asked.

"Let's have a baby," she said. I know when she's kidding, and I knew this was not one of those times. Maybe she'd been out in the sun too long.

"Have you lost your mind? Why would you even suggest such a thing?"

"It's not as crazy as it sounds. I want to have a baby. Neither one of us wants to raise one, so I say we have one, and then we let some nice couple who can't conceive have a baby. It's a way to do something really great for someone else. Not just great, important. Can you imagine doing anything greater that would make such a difference in someone else's lives? Do you know how many deserving couples out there go through hell trying to adopt kids? It would be a win-win for everyone." I hadn't seen her this excited since she cleaned up at darts at the Oasis on Sunday Funday. I was also puzzled as to why suddenly Anson was out of the running in this grand scheme. I admit my ego seemed especially satisfied that I had once again beaten him at something else. And this was a lot bigger than gin rummy or beer pong.

"So you and I would create a baby and sell it on eBay? Are you visiting Lorene on her planet today? Tell me, what's it like there?"

"I'm serious. This could be our chance to do something really noble and amazing for someone else. And we're not selling anything on eBay. We just find some deserving couple who wants a baby, and we provide one for them. A totally unselfish act. This is incredible," she said.

"I agree. Incredible as in 'How incredible! Jamie's lost her mind'."

She was persistent. "Would you at least think about it? Think about it overnight and let me know tomorrow when you get here. My God, maybe this is why we were supposed to meet."

"Supposed to meet?" I asked.

"I believe things happen for a reason. I believe in signs. I don't think there is any such thing as a coincidence. Everything about us was leading us up to this moment and this decision. Don't you think that's unbelievable?"

"Yeah, I think unbelievable pretty much sums it up."

Suddenly I felt like I needed to leave. I stood up and started gathering my stuff.

"Where are you going? You just got here," said Jamie.

"I have a ton of things I have to get done," I said. "I'll see you tomorrow." I couldn't get over how serious she was about the idea of having a baby with me. Maybe it was one of her more inventive pranks, and she would have a good laugh on me tomorrow. Why was I feeling my stomach in a knot at the prospect that she was serious? Why would she want to do this with me and not one of the others from her collection of possibilities? Why did we forget to tell Lorene that the whole selling-a-baby-on-eBay was just a joke? Big oversight.

CHAPTER SEVEN – "ABC"

Michael Olsen stared into the bathroom mirror at the spot he had missed shaving. Years ago he would have started from scratch and reshaved his entire face. That was back when he was desperately trying to climb his way up the ladder at the studio and had to appear perfect for the executives he was spending every waking minute trying to impress. It had taken a few years, but he was now in a position high enough to be the one others were out to dazzle. He took his Fusion and did a quick swipe across the errant patch of stubble on the lower left side of his chin. He was back to being more meticulous these days. There were still higher-ups he had to answer to daily, and lately their patience with his productivity seemed strained. The last two weekly staff meetings were full of the usual talk of sponsors, ratings, and the routine number crunching reports. Still, he was aware of the underlying tension when it came his turn to fill them in on the progress of his development team. He had been in new program development for four years, and two years ago he had been promoted to director of reality programming. It was his dream job. Michael loved reality TV, plain and simple. His idea for *Celebrity Shopper* had taken off and boosted his stock tremendously, probably earning him the position he was now in. He got the idea when he was buying a tie at a boutique on Rodeo Drive and was waiting in line at the counter. The smartly dressed woman in front of him was telling her daughter that if she didn't have exactly the right color of shirt for Mr. Kutcher, she'd have to hear about it for at least an hour. Michael figured there weren't that many Kutcher's in Hollywood sending personal assistants out to buy $400 shirts, and took an educated guess that she was referring to Ashton Kutcher.

Ashton had been approached by ABC a number of times with open offers for development deals. His success with *Punk'd* had made him a logical target for networks who were hoping he could make lightning strike a second time for them. Michael had taken a meeting with Ashton on one such occasion, only to be politely told that he was pretty much over the *Punk'd* phase and getting back to acting one hundred percent of the time. Michael was hoping the good rapport he had established during one short meeting would allow him a second chance to run a new idea past him. It was worth a phone call.

"Hi, it's Michael Olsen from ABC. We met just a few months ago, and I ran some ideas past you."

"Sure, I remember. Same answer as before. Too busy for anything new," Ashton politely replied.

"Well, I just happen to have this new idea, and you were kind of the inspiration for it, so I felt obligated to bring it to you first." Michael held his breath during the pause that followed. Then a response came.

"Really? And how did I so unknowingly provide you with this…idea?"

"I was in a shop today on Rodeo, and I overheard someone buying you a shirt. I heard her say you'd be sore as hell if it wasn't the right thing. I'm sure she was just joking." Michael added the last part quickly, not wanting to get the assistant in trouble and not wanting to imply that there might be any truth to Ashton having some sort of short temper."

"Yeah, that was Lisa, an assistant at my production company. Not a big deal. I yell at her all the time, and she yells right back. So what's your idea?"

"I'm thinking we put personal shoppers at some of the big name stores around L.A. We feed some celebrity clients into these places. They get free stuff and exposure with no time commitment longer than a shopping trip. There are enough B- listers who'd do it for the screen time, and probably some A-listers who'd just do it for fun. You kind of opened the door for celebrities willing to let the world see them as they really are. I'm sure America would love to see you go off on Lisa for getting you the wrong color shirt. And they'd put the ratings through the roof if they could watch Lisa giving it right back to you. I'm thinking of calling it *Celebrity Shopper*."

Four days later *Celebrity Shopper* was in development with Ashton Kutcher and Michael Olsen as executive producers.

Was it possible that ABC didn't even plan to give Michael time to catch his breath before coming up with the next great American reality television show? Reality shows were taking over the networks and he guessed the pressure to find the newest best thing was the reason he was being paid the kind of salary he was getting. He was one of the few "nice guys" in this business who were far outnumbered by the cutthroat executives who would sell their mothers for a hit show. He must have earned some decent Karma along the way, because the key to his biggest success yet would soon be sitting beside him at the media dinner/fundraiser he was attending the following evening.

It was one of those times when you wonder if there isn't something to the idea of destiny or fate or whatever you might want to call it. When Michael arrived at the dinner, he was annoyed when he and his girlfriend Lili were escorted to their table, only to find there were no empty seats. It would have been a great table for networking with the likes of Katie Couric and Ryan Seacrest. Lili, a big Seacrest fan, squeezed Michaels's arm in protest when he agreed to be seated at a different table. They followed the pretty hostess back to the entrance where she checked a seating chart on a podium near the door. She apologized for the error, explaining that somehow some seats had been reassigned after the tickets to the soiree had been sent out. Michael knew exactly what had happened. The extensive erasures on the chart were the result of several pushy Hollywood types vying to get "preferred seating." Lili had a look on her face that displayed her dissatisfaction with the way he so easily acquiesced to their relocation. Glancing at the name placards on the table, he noticed that most of his dinner companions were non show business types. It might actually be a refreshing change of pace not to be talking shop or feeling like he was in competition to impress others at the table. He felt bad Lili was disappointed, but his mind was in creative mode which had him distracted from his surroundings. He had a fairly unique way of trying to develop new ideas, something he thought of as his "two extremes." The first extreme meant he would run scenario after scenario through his head of all kinds of possibilities for a new show that would capture viewer attention. In order to compete with the myriad of reality shows, it needed to have staying power as well. *Survivor* was such an example. Season after season it endured, with only a change of location and a few new gimmicks for each pair of tribes that were plunked down onto some exotic, remote locale. Right now his mind was drifting to the place it always did when he ran this show through his head. Why hadn't he come up with something that would allow him to do his job in a tropical paradise? He mentally kicked himself every time he visited the thought.

He was almost through the exhausting stage of running possibilities through his head. Tonight's not-so-brilliant ideas included a show highlighting people with weird occupations, then people who were down on their luck and were given some kind of benevolent intervention to fix their lives, and last of all he analyzed a storyline following lottery winners to see how a gigantic monetary windfall changed their lives.

Each time he drew the same conclusion. These had already been done in some way, shape, or, form. But he also knew that as soon as he wasn't looking, some crazy new show involving Kardashians or trash hoarders would burst onto a network and remind the industry that America would buy just about any ludicrous notion that was set in front of them. This recurring thought was frustrating because it only meant one thing. His job should be easier than it was.

He ordered drinks and moved onto phase two. Lili was used to him entering this strange reverie into which he'd retreat for awhile. She knew it didn't last too long, and he would emerge in a much better mood if she didn't interrupt him or demand his attention. Stage two was what he called "the blank page." He would let his mind go completely blank and wait for something, anything that might be a viable programming possibility. Tonight, absolutely nothing appeared on the page. Maybe there were just too many distractions. As he was drifting back to the table, he noticed the entire table was laughing. Some were shaking their heads and wiping their eyes. He must have missed quite a joke. For a brief moment he worried that perhaps someone had spoken to him while he was far off in his own thoughts. Were they laughing at him?

Lili was there to help him out. "Do you believe that, Honey?" she asked.

"I'm sorry. I was thinking of something, and I missed it. What did I miss?"

"Earth to Olsen," laughed the junior executive

seated to Michael's right. "I was just relating one of the crazier things that happened at work today." Michael glanced toward the man's wine glass and saw his placard with "Steven Rosenfeld, eBay" neatly written in gold calligraphy.

"Oh, and what was that?" Michael politely asked, hoping it wouldn't irritate the others at the table who had already had a good laugh at the story.

"Well, I was just telling them that some girl from Pennsylvania had contacted Customer Support today with a question. It seems some friends of hers upset her because they were considering selling their baby on eBay. I thought it was a nut job or a prank. We've gotten some bizarre questions through our support department, but never this."

"So what happened?" Michael asked. He wasn't even aware that his left knee started bouncing to some silent, quick, rhythmic beat, but Lili noticed it and put her hand on his knee to stop it.

"Damn it, I should have saved the printout our tech guy showed me with the whole conversation. The girl who wrote in to Support wouldn't drop it. Insisted her friends were just the kind of people who would do this. My tech guy assured her it was illegal, and it would never happen. Someone must have put her up to it because that's when she went over the edge with the joke."

"How so?" asked Michael. The knee started jack hammering again.

"Get this. She said they weren't doing it for the money. They wanted to sell it just to help someone out who couldn't have a baby."

"Maybe she was serious. About her friends, I mean," Lili said with a smile. "I'd like to think not everybody does things just for money."

Her sincere comment reflecting her belief in the innate goodness of people brought another huge laugh from everyone at the table except Michael. She must have momentarily forgotten where she was and with whom she was seated.

Rosenfeld responded, "Darlin', anyone whacked out enough to try to sell a baby over the Internet is in it for the cash or the publicity."

Everyone murmured in agreement and the table's focus turned quickly to a heated debate of Kindle versus Nook. Lili had recently purchased Michael a Kindle Fire for his birthday and was waiting to hear him chime in to praise the gift she had given him. She glanced at him and saw the familiar look in his eyes, something akin to a "Do Not Disturb" sign. She took over and jumped into the discussion. "I bought Michael the Kindle Fire for his birthday recently, and he hardly ever puts it down. I swear he can't even go to the john without it." More laughter.

Suddenly Steven Rosenfeld slid his chair back and stood up. "I can't sit here all night and wait for another martini. I'm going to the bar."

Before he even turned to go, Michael stood and said, "I'll join you, Steven. Lili, a Grey Goose and soda?"

At the bar, Michael waited until their drinks were ordered before asking Steven the question he'd been waiting to ask for a good ten minutes. "So, Steven, there's something I want to ask you. I can't get over that story you told about the nut job and her baby-selling friends. You said there was a printout circulating in your office."

"Yeah, why?" asked Steven as he threw a hundred dollar bill on the bar. "Yours are on me," he told Michael.

It crossed Michael's mind that very moment that he should be the one paying for the drinks. It was the least he could have done for the guy who had given him the million dollar idea that was spinning in his head.

"Thanks. I'll get the next ones. Well, you know I'm at ABC, and we're always looking for that kind of crazy shit to stick in shows. There's gotta be some way I could turn this into a funny bit, like maybe get this girl on the phone with Jimmy Kimmel some night during his monologue. Can you help me out?"

"My wife's a big fan of *Celebrity Shopper*. She'd kill me if I didn't do you such a simple favor. That is your show, isn't it?"

Michael gave a modest shrug and smiled, "Guilty."

"All our Customer Support communications stay in our system for at least a month, but duh, I just realized I probably have the printout still sitting on my desk. It'll have a contact e-mail address on it. It was someone named Maureen or Lorraine or something like that. I'll fax it to you first thing tomorrow. Got a card?"

It was a question of mere formality since everyone in the room had his card in his pocket just as sure as he was wearing socks. Michael handed over the card and for good measure added, "Thanks. I owe you one." Those last four words were not spoken lightly in this town. They proceeded back to the table with the drinks just as Caesar salads were being placed at each setting.

"What's going on?" whispered Lili. "I thought your shoe was going to come flying off a few minutes ago. That means you're onto something."

"It's nothing really. I'll tell you later."

"Michael, I know you, and I know when you're excited about something. Your knee is a dead giveaway."

"You're going to have to wait at least until we're in the car, and then I'll tell you. Let's just enjoy dinner, ok? It can wait till later."

Michael enjoyed the salad and the filet he had ordered. But he never touched his drink again. He didn't want alcohol disrupting the flood of ideas that was being sorted and categorized in his head. By the time dessert arrived, he had mentally rejected dozens of his own ideas, but also committed even more to memory. It took all of his will power to refrain from entering these ideas on his smartphone. He would have to trust his memory. This is what he was great at, and what lie ahead excited him more than anything he could imagine. He likely would be up all night mapping out the show that was quickly taking form in his brain. Lili knew something was up and just let him go with it. The rest of the table was either too self-absorbed or getting too drunk to notice that he had closed himself off from communication with them. He occasionally would smile and nod in the direction of whoever was speaking, but he never heard a word.

CHAPTER EIGHT – "THE DEAL"

When the phone rings before seven in the morning it means one of two things: either it snowed like a bitch the night before and school was cancelled, or it meant that someone needed a ride to work. I figured it had to be the second reason because it was September, and we were still in the dog days of summer. Our school building had new carpeting in the halls, renovated science labs, and a football field that cost a small fortune. It did not have air conditioning. I guess the school board figured that kids wouldn't be suffering inside the school during the summer, but failed to take into account the fact that temperatures could feasibly hit the 70's and even the 80's in May or September.

The voice on the other end was unfamiliar but introduced itself immediately as Michael Olsen from ABC. Being early in the morning I was still a little foggy and assumed it was someone from the local affiliate. I knew some people at the local TV station, but I'd never heard of a Michael Olsen before.

My response probably sounded a little rude, but I'd been called by my acquaintances at the station when they wanted an inside scoop whenever there was anything remotely controversial in the school district. One who frequently called to dig for information was Abby Taggart, a pretty news anchor I had befriended who liked to meet up with me on occasion for karaoke night. She would have known better than to call me this early, but maybe she put one of her colleagues up to it.

"I'm on my way out the door to work right now. I'm guessing you're calling because the next contract negotiations are starting, but those won't really get rolling for another couple of months," I stated firmly in an attempt to cut him off.

"That's not why I called," replied Olsen. "I really would like to talk to you about something you might be interested in. And I swear, I'm not selling anything. If I could just have your ear for about ten minutes, I think it would be worth your while."

"Sorry, I really am just heading out the door. Maybe I could talk to you after work. There's a bunch of us meeting at the Three B's, and then you'd have an entire roomful of teachers on hand to talk to."

"You don't understand. This has nothing to do with teachers. It's of a more personal nature. I'd be happy to meet with you, but that's not really convenient. I'm in California. Did I mention that I work for ABC television?"

I couldn't imagine what this total stranger could possibly have to say to me that would be "worth my while" as he put it.

My curiosity got the best of me. It might just be worth missing my morning coffee time with Jamie although she usually got pissed off when that happened.

"I have ten minutes," I said. "Go ahead. Wait a minute. First tell me how you got my phone number."

Olsen began talking, but I wasn't quite sure what

he was getting it. It had something to do with him calling Lorene and getting my phone number, and it had something to do with Jamie.

"You need to back up a second," I instructed him. "Why exactly did you call Lorene?"

Then came the unbelievable explanation. Olsen cleared his throat and began. "Your friend Lorene contacted eBay with some concern because she believed you and your girlfriend were going to try to sell your baby on eBay."

"Oh, my God, this is incredible," I said. "First of all, that was a complete joke. You'd have to know Lorene to understand. She is as sweet as she comes and obviously just as gullible. Second of all, Jamie is not my girlfriend. And third, both Jamie and I know full well that it would be illegal to try and sell a baby on eBay. Are you kidding me?"

"Of course it would," Olsen replied. "But it would be perfectly legal to have a baby and put it up for adoption, right?"

"I don't see what you have to do with this or what you're getting at. Why exactly are you calling?"

"I want you to put your baby up for adoption on national television."

There was, pardon the pun, quite the pregnant pause as I let this sink in.

"What?" was all I could say, even though I had heard him perfectly.

He spoke quickly answering all of my questions before I could even get them out. It seemed as if his sales pitch had been rehearsed long before I answered the phone.

"According to your friend, you and this Jamie want to have a baby for the sole purpose of helping out some random childless couple. I can supply you with hundreds of potential parents. Hell, I could probably get you thousands, but we only really need a handful for what I have in mind. Some people may object and think that doing this would be morally reprehensible. I want to assure you, for what it's worth, I do not feel this way. What you are doing, or what I'd like you to consider doing, is to just allow America to watch this noble, wonderful, unselfish act you were already thinking of doing anyway. You would both need to quit your jobs, but that's okay because you wouldn't be going into this without being compensated. Technically, you can't be paid for the act of making a baby and putting it up for adoption. We've already established that would be illegal. Our legal department was very clear that this can be nothing more than the televising of an adoption process that is followed to the letter of law. However, you would be credited as co-creators of the show, and I'm proposing that your "salaries" would also be covered by your work as consultants for the show. I've spent the last week clearing all of this with our legal department. I'm not going to lie, there are some tricky issues at work here, but if I'm right and I usually am, I think I've thought about every possible obstacle we might face if we get this off the ground."

"As someone who likes his fair share of television, I have to tell you, it sounds pretty boring to

105

me. Watching an adoption sounds about as exciting as watching paint dry," I offered.

"And I would agree with you, except that you haven't heard the hook."

"The hook?" I asked.

"The hook that will make millions of people feel as if they are going through this with you every step of the way. We narrow the prospective couples down each week as America votes on who gets to adopt E-baby. Each week another couple bites the dust, and the suspense goes higher...right along with the ratings."

"I don't know what to say," I stammered.

"Say nothing. You'll have time to respond to me after you speak to your girlfriend, sorry, I mean Jamie."

"Can I just ask....why us?" It wasn't a casual question. I really wanted to know.

"I'm sold on the tie-in with the whole miscommunication involving your friend Lorene and eBay. It gives the whole story that human element. That's the kind of twist that, if we publicize it right, will suck America right in. It's the gimmick, and if there's one thing I know about what I do, it's the gimmick that will make it fly or die. This thing will fly like a 747. I'm sure of it. America is going to fall in love big time with *E-baby*."

"*E-baby*? What's *E-baby*? I'm sorry, I'm a little overwhelmed," I said.

"That's going to be the name of the show. I already have eBay's blessing because they have been promised a sponsorship. This will put eBay back in the spotlight in a way it hasn't seen since its inception."

"I don't know. I'm late for work. I don't know." I sounded like a broken record.

"One last thing," continued Olsen. "I'm not trying to appeal to any sense of greed, I swear. But I do want you to realize the financial possibilities for something like this. The merchandizing division of ABC is already at work developing a line of *E-baby* products. I have the go-ahead to inform you that you and Jamie would also be entitled to a flat percentage of any merchandising connected with *E-baby*."

"You mean we get ten cents for every tee shirt that gets sold?" I asked, not quite realizing the magnitude of this latest temptation on the table.

"That's what is so incredible about this. Baby-related products are one of the biggest markets in the country. We're looking at *E-baby* clothing, *E-baby* baby food, *E-baby* diapers. A line of *E-baby* toys was discussed, not to mention my personal favorite, *E-baby* vitamins. It's a fucking gold mine. Sorry, I get a little enthusiastic," Olsen said, not sure if his profanity would offend me.

"I have to go, Mr. Olsen," I said.

"It's Michael from now on. I think I can say with confidence that we're entering a pretty exciting adventure together. I'm going to give you my work number and my cell phone. I'll be waiting for your call. One other thing, and it's very important. Please don't tell anyone about this except Jamie. Anything can happen until papers are signed, and this entire project is a closely guarded secret right now at the network. You understand, right?"

"Of course," I responded. Not having a clue how rare it was for anyone to get these two personal phone numbers, I took down the numbers he gave me and rushed to my car. I was going to be late, but it's not like someone couldn't cover me until I got there. A crazy thought flew through my head. Let them fire me. Right now all I had in my brain were images of palm trees, and movie premiers, and sitting by a swimming pool playing backgammon with Jamie. Pool Party was moving to Hollywood! It felt like what I imagined hitting a million dollars on a scratch-off ticket would feel like. It was surreal.

It wasn't until I slowed to a stop at a red light, that I came back to earth long enough to realize there was one little detail I hadn't mentioned to my new friend Michael. There was no baby.

Jamie thought there was something wrong when I opened her classroom door twenty minutes later and asked to speak with her in the hall. "Ms. Jernigan, could I possibly see you out here for a minute?" I asked, as if a minute would cover it.

"I'm just getting this class started on creating a color wheel. Why don't you wait in my office, and I'll be right in," she said in her most professional teacher voice.

I did what she asked, taking a seat at her desk. The three minutes it took her to join me in her office seemed like forever.

When she finally came in and closed the door, she said, "Let me sit there so I can watch them through the window. This bunch likes to talk too much, and I might need to go keep them in line." I pulled a chair over toward her desk and transferred to it. "What's up with you? You look like you're ready to freak out. Does this have something to do with why you weren't down here this morning?"

As excited as I was to tell her about Michael Olsen and *E-baby*, I wanted to make sure she didn't get too weirded out by what I was about to say. I also wanted to savor the entire process of relating the proposal to her. I knew she would think I was joking, so I began speaking in my most serious voice.

"What I'm about to tell you is not bullshit. Please try not to interrupt me." I could tell by the look on her face that she believed me. There was mostly a look of concern, like she was afraid I was about to announce that I had cancer.

Because I couldn't resist, I went for the dramatic. "How would you like to be rich? Not just rich, but famous too. What would you say if I told you I wanted you to quit your job and move to California? And how would you feel about it knowing that I'd be there too? Both of us. Rich and living in California. And famous."

Jamie stared at me for a second before she responded. "How rich?" was all she asked.

"I don't know. Really rich. Let's just say really rich."

The story of Michael Olsen's phone call came spilling out of me. The kids on the other side of the door could have been painting each other with fluorescent paint and it probably wouldn't have fazed Jamie.

I could tell by the way she was shaking her head that she already thought of the major obstacle standing between us and fame and fortune. "I know. There's no baby," I said. "That seems huge, but there's got to be some way to figure this out. The obvious thing would be to get you pregnant somehow."

"Somehow?" she laughed. "Maybe you'd better go upstairs and sit in on Marty's health class for awhile."

"You know what I meant! Do you think it's as crazy as it sounds?" I asked.

Suddenly Jamie got uncharacteristically quiet and serious. "It sounds to me like we're back to the original joke about selling a baby. I can't do that. It sounds glamorous and all, but really?"

"I thought that too, at first. But while this Michael Olsen was pitching this to me, in a very hard-sell way I might add, he used the word 'adventure.' Suddenly it seemed okay to me. Nothing has really changed about the end result of all this. We would be giving some deserving couple the gift of a lifetime."

"I can't believe they'd really be able to put this on television," Jamie mused, mentally inching closer to the place where she believed this could really happen.

"Michael assured me that ABC's legal department

has it all covered. Listen to that. ABC's legal department. Who would ever have believed we'd be sitting here talking about ABC's legal department?"

"We need to come back to reality. How much time do I have to get pregnant?"

"Yeah, about that. You see, I think Michael thinks you're already pregnant."

"What?" Her voiced was raised in disbelief.

"Yeah, I think Lorene's message to eBay must have made them assume you were already on your way. But right when he was giving me his phone number, he said something about us being out there within a month when everything was ready to be gone over, discussed, and signed on the dotted line. He's still dealing with all kinds of red tape, which is good because it gives us time to get you to a sperm bank."

"Nope," was all she said.

"Nope, what?"

"They'd find out somehow, don't you think? I think they're expecting a couple that's having a baby...together. As in real parents. I think it has to be you and me."

"So you want to use my stuff and do some kind of in vitro fertilization?"

"There's no time for that," Jamie said. She smiled and raised her eyebrows twice.

"Whoa there. I struck out in that department before. You know that. Our odds would suck. I think you're dreaming if you think you can get knocked up that fast."

"If we were playing the Powerball I'd agree. We'd

have better odds of both of us getting struck by lightning on the same day. But me getting pregnant? Much better odds, trust me."

"This is ridiculous. Who are we kidding?"

"You know I believe in signs. Right before you came to the door, I was talking primary and secondary colors with the class. I asked what color came in between blue and violet, and Cindy, the girl in the front seat of the second row, guessed baby blue. Baby blue? We can do this!" Jamie's confidence didn't make it sound any less crazy.

"So the discussion of this is over? Just like that? You think it's going to be that easy?" I couldn't believe this was happening.

"No. I still have one question," she said. "Your place or mine?"

"Oh, my God."

"That's right," Jamie said with a huge smile. "Start praying. I'm at just the right time of the month, and I'm feeling good and creative if you know what I mean."

"Your place," was all I said as I walked out of her office.

CHAPTER NINE – "THE FIRST DATE"

I had no idea what to expect as I pulled into the parking lot and took a space right in front of Jamie's apartment that evening. This was maybe the strangest I had ever felt in my life. All day long my stomach alternately registered something between excitement and fear. I was used to not knocking on her door whenever I came over. I would always just walk in and scold her for never locking her door. I quietly opened the door and timidly entered directly into the kitchen of her apartment. There were some covered pans on the stove, and I could smell something baking in the oven. It smelled great, but I was pretty sure the knot in my gut would prevent me from eating anything.

I could hear her stereo in the living room. It wasn't blasting the usual Bon Jovi I was accustomed to hearing at her place. This was something quieter, and I strained my ears to determine what it was. It was Faith Hill. I didn't even think Jamie owned a Faith Hill album, despite the fact she knew I was a huge fan. Jamie wasn't selfish by nature, but at her place she was picky about what got played on her CD player. In a stubborn standoff, I refused to ever play Bon Jovi at my place. I noticed there were flowers on the table, not part of her usual decorating scheme. The table was set with real dishes, not the brightly colored plastic ones she used for every day. I knew this was all for me, and I suddenly regretted not having brought the bottle of Merlot I had been saving for when it was my turn to cook for her at my place. The thought had crossed my mind that alcohol, even a glass of wine was not a good idea this evening. The goal here was to have peak performance to maximize our chances of conception, and I wasn't going to risk anything by drinking.

Jamie turned the corner from the living room and saw me standing in the middle of her kitchen.

"Hey, hot stuff. Buy a girl a drink?" she said in a deep voice.

I got the irony of this immediately. No matter what I did, or didn't do, or said, I was going to get lucky tonight.

"I almost brought a bottle of Merlot. I could go get it. I just thought maybe I shouldn't start drinking because, well, you know."

"Not a problem," she said. "I have some Pinot Grigio in the fridge. I got it to go with the chicken." She retrieved the bottle from the refrigerator door and refilled the almost-empty glass I had just noticed sitting next to her toaster oven. "Do you want some?"

"No, I'm good," I replied. "But go ahead. You probably should relax."

"I'm not really drinking this to relax. It's got more to do with being freaked out. Okay. Let's get the weirdness out of the way. Let's just approach this like two adults who are going to enjoy each other's company for a few nights this week."

My question as to whether this was going to be a

one-night thing had just been answered. I was trying to think of something funny to say to ease the tension, but Jamie beat me to it.

"I hope you don't think you're getting dinner every time, though. This is just in honor of opening night," she said in a phony serious voice.

"No way," I shot back. "Do you think I'm some kind of cheap slut? If you want some of this," I said swinging my hips at her, "you're gonna buy me dinner every time. Maybe even a movie."

Jamie carried the plates to the stove where she proceeded to dish up dinner. She reached into the oven with a fork and stabbed a piece of chicken covered in bread crumbs and placed it on one of the plates. "One for me," she said. She reached in a second time for another piece of chicken and put it on the other plate. "And one for you." Next she gave us each a scoop of Stove Top stuffing and a neat row of fresh green beans on each plate. It didn't escape my notice that this meal was at the top of my list of dinners she knew I liked.

The dinner started, complete with awkward small talk.

"This is really good," I said. I was having trouble swallowing the food. I went to the refrigerator and brought back a two-liter bottle of Diet Dr Pepper to help wash down each bite. As I poured myself a glass, I offered some to her.

"No thanks, I'll just stick with the wine," she politely replied.

We pushed our food around for a few minutes

with occasional attempts at normal conversation about school and how the rest of our day had been. I realized that we were just drifting away from each other and feeling more awkward and decided to bring the focus back to where it needed to be.

"I talked to Michael Olsen after work," I informed her.

"Really? What did you say?"

"I told him we were 99 percent sure we were in. He sounded a little disappointed that we didn't fully commit, but I wanted to leave an escape hatch open in case things, you know, don't work out."

"You are so freakin' smart," Jamie said, and it boosted my confidence to hear her say that. "What's next? Beside what's happening next upstairs, I mean," she said.

"He said he'd stay in touch. He went on some more about how the wheels are in motion and how happy he is that we're on board. He can't wait to meet us. He also thinks we're both attractive enough to create even more interest with a viewing audience."

"How would he know that?"

"I wondered the same thing. He creeped our Facebook walls, and I friended him before I came over here tonight. By the way, you need to accept his friend request as soon as possible. I'm sure he's already sent it to you."

"That seems kind of weird," Jamie commented. "We don't even really know this guy."

"Well, if things go as planned, get ready. Our lives will be an open book to him. But my instincts tell me that he's okay. He's definitely a smooth talker, but there's something about him that makes me think we can trust him."

"I'll take your word for it," Jamie said. "I don't think I can eat anymore of this."

"Me neither. I think we need to just get down to what we're here for. I'm sorry. Did that sound really stupid or inconsiderate?"

"No. I know what you mean. Do you want to come upstairs?"

"Sure. Want me to clean up here first?"

"No, it'll give me something to do after you leave," she said.

My other question had just been answered. I was not spending the night. And why would I? This was all business. Well, mostly business. It's not like there wasn't a certain amount of affection between us. Part of me had thought she might have wanted me to stay, but I guess I was wrong. It probably would have made the night even weirder than it was already on track to be.

"Can we leave Faith Hill on?" I asked as we made our way to the stairs.

"Sure. I picked it up on my way home this afternoon. I figured you'd like it."

"Aww, that's really sweet," I said.

"I know. I'm sweet."

We were silent the rest of the way to her bedroom. I had only been in that room once before when she asked me to help her carry some books up to her closet. When we got to her room she sat down on the far side of the bed with her back to me. I took my place on the other side of the bed and carefully removed my shoes and socks and placed them next to her night stand.

"Would you mind if I kept most of my clothes on?" she asked. I had seen her in a bikini almost every day of the summer, but I understood her sudden shyness.

"Whatever you want," I said.

She got under the covers and proceeded to take her jeans off and drop them on the floor beside the bed. I crossed to the doorway and flipped the light switch, surprised at how completely dark the room was. "Is that okay?" I asked.

"Whatever you want," she said.

I dropped my jeans on the floor, fumbled in the dark toward the bed, and climbed in wearing just my Nike tee shirt and underwear.

"So..." began Jamie, slowly exhaling audibly. "Let's just do this and not be weird about it."

"That sounds like a good plan," I responded. Neither one of us moved. "I kind of feel like I need to say something. Are we sure we want to do this? Not the whoopee part, but the whole *E-baby* thing."

"I'm okay with it if you are."

"Then I am too. As long as we don't get too disappointed, if the results aren't..." I let the rest of the sentence drift out into the dark room.

"Oh, it'll happen," she said with full conviction in her voice. "How do you want to get started?"

"Maybe you could rub my back. Massage is the

most common form of foreplay. Not that I expect that we have a lot of foreplay. I just meant it might be…"

"Oh, for God's sake, shut up!" Jamie laughed and rolled over on top of me and started massaging my shoulders. The fact that she suddenly took charge really didn't surprise me. "You know, I think we should make them put us up in the swankiest hotel they can find out there. Do you think we'll be in Hollywood, or L.A., or maybe Beverly Hills?"

"I don't know. I've never been there." I got quiet for a moment as I concentrated on her hands working my shoulders into submission. "How can you be so sure of everything?" I wondered out loud.

"I had another sign," she replied. "It came this afternoon when I stopped at Wegmans to buy dinner and the flowers. I was going to stick one of those little cards on the flowers with some smart-ass comment about making you dinner in exchange for you making me pregnant."

"I didn't see any card," I interrupted.

"That's because there wasn't one. I reached into their little plastic tray for a card, and the first one I picked had little ducks on it and said 'Congratulations on Your New Little One'. I put it back and moved right to the checkout."

"And that's the sign that you'll get pregnant? Congratulations on your new little one?"

"It either meant that, or it was a rude comment on your penis size," she said laughing.

"Well then," was all I could think to say.

It was very nice. It was very quiet. It didn't take

long, but it didn't feel like 'Wham, bam, thank you ma'am.' It was kind of like we were starting on a trip together, and the first stop was really amazing. Like what you would imagine seeing the Grand Canyon for the first time is probably like. I shared my analogy with her, and I could tell she was smiling even though it was still dark as ever in the room.

After we were finished, we lay side by side in silence for a good twenty minutes. I was wide awake, my thoughts racing. Jamie was so quiet I thought maybe she had fallen asleep. Suddenly she sat up and started to get dressed. "Well, I guess I'll see you tomorrow at work. Are you gonna get your ass there in time for coffee with me in the morning?" she asked.

She walked me downstairs and to the door, and for a fleeting moment I thought it might be appropriate to give her a goodnight kiss. There seemed nothing in her demeanor that indicated she expected such a gesture, so I stepped through the doorway and turned to say goodnight.

"Thanks for the backgammon," she said. "Do you want a rematch tomorrow?"

I realized she was speaking in code so I played along. "Sure," I said.

"Same time, same place?" she asked.

"Sure. I'll bring dinner," I offered.

"Nah, don't worry about it. Or if you want, how about picking up two flatbread Subways and some Doritos? It'll be like Pool Party only indoors, and it's just us."

"Deal," I said.

We made two more stops for backgammon, so to speak, on our trip together that week. Niagara Falls and Mount Rushmore. Both amazing places.

In retrospect, they were just bonus stops because when Jamie handed me a cup of coffee weeks later in her office one morning and announced calmly that we made a baby, she added that she was pretty sure it happened the very first time at the Grand Canyon.

CHAPTER TEN – "THE MOVE"

Michael Olsen lost no time getting us moved out to California. Jamie's boys were puzzled as to why she was moving across the country with her best friend, but she wasn't ready to fill them in yet on the strange details involving this sudden upheaval. Darrell, who insisted the "Little" be dropped from his name long ago, was wrapped up in his romance and watching from the sidelines as his fiancé planned their wedding. All he cared about was that Jamie be home for the big day. She assured him that there was nothing on earth that would keep her from being there on her first son's wedding day.

Vincent was in college and extremely self-sufficient, a trait he had obviously gotten from his mother. His life was completely absorbed in studying and working, and he called her just once a week even though she would have preferred it to be more frequently.

We both gave up our apartments and jointly threw the things we weren't taking into storage. No one at school knew what to make of the double departure of two faculty members at the same time. We were in strict agreement that the less said, the better. Our pat answer was that we were moving out to California because we had found an opportunity to go into business there together. Everyone bought it. It happened so quickly we dodged any big going away parties. They did decide to throw us a going away happy hour at the Three B's after our last day of work.

Fran, a social studies teacher who was the stereotypical school marm, approached us as soon as we walked through the door of the bar. She was determined to get some information out of us, and began by trying to pin down our relationship.

"So what is it with you two?" she asked. "I heard you two were thick as thieves all summer, but I didn't know that it had gone this far."

"How far is that?" asked Jamie, glancing at me and rolling her eyes quickly so that Fran didn't see her.

"Quitting your jobs out of the blue and running off together. It's like something out of a romance novel. Are you getting married?" She wasn't even being subtle.

"We've both tried that. Been there, done that, so probably not," I said.

"We thought it would be much more exciting to just live in sin," Jamie added. I shot her a look to stop her, but she was having too much fun.

"So there is something to what I've been hearing in the faculty room," continued Fran. "I knew it." She took a step toward me, sloshing a little of her chardonnay onto my shoe. In a loud whisper she said directly into my face, "Everyone said you were too old for her, but I've seen the way you two act when you're together. I say, 'Go do your thing', and the heck with what anybody says. I wish I could just pack up and move somewhere warm." Fran took a slug of her wine, and I thought for a second it looked like she might be on the verge of tears. How much wine had this old broad downed before we got there?

"Thanks, Fran," I said, steering Jamie away from her toward the bar. "We'll miss you."

Something akin to that scenario was repeated over the next two hours as our colleagues came over to wish us well and fish for details. We stuck to our story, maneuvering away from any solid information. Fortunately, the more our teacher friends drank, the less they seemed to care about why we were leaving. They focused now on the simple fact we were leaving, and hugs and handshakes were thrown at us like rice at a wedding.

We arrived at the Erie airport with less than thirty minutes before takeoff. Jamie did this on purpose to prove a point. There were only a few connecting flights from Erie to Cleveland, Buffalo, Pittsburgh, Philadelphia, or Detroit. As we expected, our first plane was a puddle jumper to Cleveland that seated no more than eighteen people. Since we already downloaded our boarding passes on line, Jamie insisted we ignore the recommendation to get there an hour before departure. Her goal was to walk from the cab we took, directly to security, and then onto the plane. "Ha! See how much time we didn't waste sitting here?" she gloated.

Our bags were checked all the way through to L.A. The last time we had traveled together, we were each other's date for the destination wedding of a mutual friend. We drove to Cleveland to start the itinerary for that trip since flying out of a bigger city was a much better deal from Travelocity. Jamie insisted we jam five days worth of clothes, toiletries, books, and shoes, into carry-ons so we wouldn't have to pay for checked baggage. It was one of those things she got riled up about, and one of the things I found endearing about her. There was no such concern about checking bags this time. Everything was being paid for by ABC. We would have been in first class on the puddle jumper if such a thing existed, which it didn't. However, from Cleveland to L.A. we were in for a treat. Neither one of us had ever shelled out for first class before, and we felt like royalty.

"Oh, my God, this chocolate chip cookie is warm. They must have just come out of a freakin' oven," marveled Jamie. "And look at the magazines. I swear they're brand new. They don't have those nasty plastic covers on them that smell like barf. This is great."

I had to agree. This was the coolest way to travel, and we were getting this taste of the "high life" less than two states away from home. It only made our impending arrival in California that much more promising and exciting.

When we landed and deplaned, we walked into the terminal and headed for baggage claim. As soon as we were past the security checkpoint, we were approached by what I presumed to be our driver who seemed to recognize us immediately. I assumed Michael Olsen had shown him our pictures. He was very pleasant and introduced himself, shaking our hands after removing the black cap he was wearing.

"We're parked right outside of baggage claim. If you point out your bags, I'll have someone move them to the car," he instructed.

Jamie gave me a smile, leaned in to me, and said, "Well, la-di-da."

Once we were on our way, our driver, Mitchell, informed us that Mr. Olsen was going to let us get settled at our hotel, a place called Hotel Amarano Burbank. He would meet us later for dinner at the hotel. He thought we might need time to rest up after the trip.

Obviously, Mr. Olsen didn't anticipate how excited we were, and that we could have been ready in five minutes to go out and see the town. Once we checked into our room, we sat down on an ornate love seat near the window to catch our breath. We had requested a room with two queen sized beds. The room wasn't over-the-top fancy but had an exotic southern California feel to it that we weren't used to.

"Oh, my God, this is unbelievable," Jamie said.

"I know. I wonder how long they're going to put us up here. I keep thinking we're going to find out that this is some kind of elaborate joke, and the real show is going to be about how we crumble when we find out this is all pretend."

"It's not though. Did Michael tell you that we get our own lawyer tomorrow when we sign on for the show? And they pay for it. I guess they're paying for pretty much everything. I can't believe this is happening."

"You never say anything about how you're feeling. I mean, there are times I forget that we're here because you're carrying a baby. How are you?" I hadn't meant to put a wet blanket on our arrival, but in an odd way, I felt the need to remind ourselves that we were here under incredibly unique circumstances to perform an ordinary function in a most unusual way. The thought was so convoluted I didn't even try to say it out loud to Jamie. She had gotten the point anyway.

"I'm ready for this. I know that mentally and emotionally it's going to be tough at times to face what we're doing. But I'm prepared. I still believe this is happening for a reason, and that thought keeps me from doubting the decision we made."

"Then let's go to dinner and schmooze Michael Olsen into putting us in the penthouse of the Beverly Hills Hilton."

"Unlikely," replied Jamie. "That's over on the other side of the hill where the big Hollywood sign stands."

"How do you know these things?" I said, impressed to discover that her trivia knowledge included more than just 80's rock bands. Her ability to name the title and artist of songs on the radio was truly impressive. Of course, it always turned into a competition when she would yell out the song title and the performer whenever we were anywhere there was a radio playing. Driving in the car was one thing, but this game even happened in restaurants which could get pretty embarrassing because her need to do this bordered on compulsion.

"The first thing I did when Michael called me with the travel arrangements was to Google the hotel. And you know me. Of course I had to check out some of the other ones around here. Pretty swanky place, eh?" said Jamie.

"I think we need to keep our heads on straight when it comes to the money. If it's as much as Michael is insinuating, we're going to have to keep from getting all crazy."

"What are you saying? I can't handle money?"

"Please. I've seen what you do when you get your extra paycheck from bartending at Applebee's on the weekends," I said teasing her. "It's gone faster than a doughnut in a cop car."

Suddenly Jamie turned serious for a moment. "You know, the money kind of makes this seem wrong. I still can't stop myself from thinking about how people might judge us. Mostly the people we know. I keep going back to worrying about how this could be turned into a moral issue, and people are going to think we're bad people for doing this."

"Did you call your parents and let them in on what you're doing? I mean, I know you must have told them you're moving, but did you tell them why?"

"I did. I knew they would tell me I'm crazy, but I figured I had to tell them."

"So what did they say?"

"They said I was crazy. Did you tell your mother?"

"Oh yeah," I answered with a tone that foreshadowed what her reaction had been. "Like you, I got the exact response I would have predicted. She informed me that if my dad was still alive this would kill him."

"See?" Jamie said. "Doing this is not going to sit well with anyone."

"People give babies up for adoption every day," I reminded her.

"But they don't get rich doing it," she responded.

"We can turn down the money," I suggested.

"Now who's talking crazy? Change your clothes and let's go eat celebrity style."

Dinner in the hotel was as gourmet as anything we had ever had. The opulent dining room was quiet, and the soft piano playing from a guy in a tuxedo at the far side of the room provided a calming effect for the rising excitement I felt as we discussed *E-baby* with Michael Olsen. He was the only person we knew out here, and he seemed trustworthy, looking out for our best interest. Somehow that automatically bonded us as friends. He had brought his girlfriend Lili with him, and we liked her immediately.

"We've really tried to think ahead and take care of everything. Even though the show will focus on the people who will be the potential adoptive parents, there will be segments each week where we follow the two of you through doctor visits and your personal interaction with each other. We've decided that you're not going to share a lot of on-screen time with the couples we follow. Some, but not a lot," Michael explained. "People will want to know everything you're doing, especially Jamie. Are you eating right? Are you taking the right vitamins?"

"So in a way we'll be educating people about proper prenatal care," Jamie said. I sensed this was springing from her money-guilt issue. She wanted America to root for her and not judge her.

"Well, don't forget this is television, and we have to keep it interesting. Sometimes interesting means controversial." Michael saw the puzzled look on our faces and continued. "Our writers already have already decided to have you bingeing on Mexican food in one episode, and being tempted to have a drink at a wedding reception in another."

"I don't understand," said Jamie. "What wedding reception are you talking about?"

"Entire daily routines and scenarios are being devised by the writing staff to give a storyline to *E-baby*. America doesn't want to just watch you eat lunch or sit and read a book. That might be the most important point I can make at our initial dinner meeting tonight. Are you ready to allow your life to be an open book? Even if it's a life we make up for you?"

"I…I guess so," Jamie said tentatively.

"How about you?" Michael asked, turning the attention to me. "Would you have a problem if we asked you to act like a jerk and walk out on your pregnant girlfriend after an argument over whose turn it is to do the dishes? I'm just making shit up now, but you get the drift, right?"

"See, there's something that's misleading right off the bat. Jamie's not my girlfriend. I told you that from the start," I reminded him.

"On *E-baby* she's your girlfriend. That's been discussed by our entire team. We debated whether or not we'd have you get married before production starts, just to make it more palatable to middle America. Of course we would have run that past you before we brought you out here, but it was decided that your marital status didn't really factor into this. This is a bold new concept, and we thought being a little edgier was the way to go. America will want to see this baby-out-of-wedlock placed into the hands of a married couple. But you and Jamie have to at least appear to be in a serious relationship for America to like you." Michael ran his eyes down the dessert menu that had just been handed to him, flipped it shut, and handed it right back to the waiter. Lili did the same, and I reasoned that people in Hollywood probably didn't eat dessert. Jamie ordered a Crème Brule.

"I understand," I said. It was at that moment I decided that if we were going to go through with this, we just needed to put our trust in Michael. I said so out loud to reassure Jamie that this was a good thing and to alleviate any anxiety she might have. I shouldn't have worried. Right now it seemed the only anxiety she had was how soon her dessert would arrive. She was eating for two after all, and I was glad she seemed a lot more at ease than when we had first sat down at the table.

"Michael is the best," offered Lili. She put her hand up to stop Michael from some kind of modest protest. "No, he really is, and I can tell you, he's not going to put either of you in some uncomfortable situation."

"I can at least promise you that there will be a balance. Anytime there is a negative, there will be a positive. It's how reality television works. We want America to embrace you. Ultimately, I plan on making *E-baby* the feel-good show of the decade. So what do you say?" Michael gave a discreet nod to the waiter who was placing Jamie's dessert in front of her, indicating that he was ready for the check.

"We're in," I replied, looking toward Jamie to make sure we were in agreement.

"Absolutely," said Jamie through a mouthful of Brule.

CHAPTER ELEVEN – "THE PILOT"

If we were from the Midwest, I would have said we were in hog heaven. At ABC studios, a roomful of men and women in suits sat us down and went over an endless list of details surrounding our participation in this thing called *E-baby*. Timing was everything for a show of this nature, and it couldn't have worked out better for us. They didn't want to start any filming until Jamie was showing, and that provided them with the opportunity to get all of the preproduction taken care of. It gave us the chance to settle into the apartment they found for us in West Hollywood. It wasn't fancy, but it was comfortable and nice. It was quiet enough and "open" enough to allow a camera crew room to do the necessary filming once we got to that point.

Jamie was thrilled when Michael's assistant, Monica, asked her if she wanted to go shopping with her and the set people whose job was to make sure that our lives were camera-ready. They didn't always allow Jamie to have her way, but she had fun decorating an entire apartment and not having to spend a penny of her own money. She picked out a tasteful leather couch, but one set designer shook his head and said, "Too shiny."

"Anyway," explained Monica, "we don't want to get too lavish. The viewer has to identify with you." At least she asked Jamie for her approval when she suggested a smaller solid blue sofa with accent pillows.

"That's nice," agreed Jamie, "but what about the plaid one over there?"

"Too busy," the designer muttered in a monotone voice.

This went on all day, but when they were finished the entire apartment was furnished, even down to the dishes and silverware we would be using.

We had almost five weeks to wait until filming would begin on *E-baby*. The studio leased a car for us, and we decided to spend our first couple of days as tourists. Michael wanted us to check in often with him, especially if there was a day when we weren't scheduled to be at the studio for some kind of preproduction work. Every once in a while, Michael would take the initiative and check in with us to see how things were going. Did we need anything? Was the apartment okay? Our only complaint was that we weren't used to the traffic in L.A. and we really didn't know our way around very well. The next day Mitchell showed up accompanied by someone who was there to retrieve the rental car we had been given.

"From now on Mr. Olsen just wants you to call whenever you need a ride somewhere. It'll probably be me who shows up. He must like you. Not everyone gets this kind of star treatment," confided Mitchell.

I called Michael that afternoon to thank him for the gesture. He said something about it being the least the studio could do for us, but I had no doubt that he was the one who saw to it that we had a driver at our disposal. Then he asked if we wanted to join him and Lili for dinner that evening. Not yet having had the opportunity to really meet anybody else, we took them up on any chance to get out and socialize. Right now they seemed to be our only contact with other people. It was Lili who pointed out that very soon we would have trouble walking down the street or going into a store without being recognized as "the people on *E-baby*." Occasionally some of the technicians from ABC would show up to experiment with lighting or to rearrange things in the apartment, but they were all business and showed no interest in us personally. Jamie did hit it off with a young woman from wardrobe who was assigned to be her personal dresser. Jamie's clothing needs would change as the show progressed, and rumor had it that a line of *E-baby* maternity clothing was already in the works. Her new friend's name was Linda, and she pointed out that soon, pregnant women all over America would be wearing whatever Jamie had on from the most recent week's episode.

I found the production details to be fascinating. Hundreds of couples had responded to the simple ad that had been placed on-line seeking married partners interested in adopting a baby under the auspices of a reality show. After an initial screening via an on-line survey, the number of couples was quickly reduced to 107 who met the basic requirements. A social worker with a PhD was hired only two days after *E-baby* was given the green light, and was now on board as a consultant, overseeing the screening at every step. The big concern of the network was to make sure that every move was legal. Nothing would halt production faster than someone claiming there was any move that wasn't completely above board.

Jenny McCreary, a popular Los Angeles based reporter for *Entertainment News*, was the final choice for the host of the show. Michael explained to me that it was a huge break for her career. Some bigger names were considered, but all of the males were dismissed from consideration. There was much more empathy on display when the female candidates screen tested by mock-interviewing several of the writers who posed as potential adoptive parents. The last few candidates were not given any script to work from. Almost every one of them ended with some pat query about what the future would hold for the couple's child. Would he someday be president? Would she someday change the world? The schmaltz reading was off the charts. Jenny McCreary's wrap up began with a referral to global warming that caused everyone to unconsciously do the old eye roll. But suddenly her eyes filled with tears that somehow managed to cling on for dear life to the surface of her eyeballs. Even the camera man was visibly choked up when Jenny's voice broke on her final question about how parents today might raise a new generation of young people to be more "gentle to the earth." The impressive thing was that the interview was all pretend. It would be even more spellbinding when it was for real.

A team was forming that included Michael, Jenny, the social worker Dr. Emily Bauschard, and two writers. Jamie and I felt left out, but Michael kept assuring us that our input would become more sought after when the show actually began filming.

We learned that we would be in the pilot episode only briefly. The real focus of the pilot and the next two episodes that followed would be on narrowing down the couples to the final nine who would vie for adopting *E-baby*. Cameras followed us around the apartment for several days to capture scenes of us in our daily lives. It seemed much less awkward than I had anticipated. After a couple of hours and having been told dozens of times not to stare at the cameras, Jamie and I learned to ignore them. There was the occasional slip like when Jamie looked directly into the camera and asked if anyone minded if she went to the bathroom. Another time, I turned around from the refrigerator and plowed full-on into a cameraman who had a portable camera hoisted onto his shoulder. I was concentrating on carrying too much at once: a carton of eggs, a half-gallon of orange juice, a large jar of grape jelly, and a loaf of bread. I never even saw the guy, and everything I was carrying hit the floor when our bodies collided. I guess we could do no wrong. They had explained the magic of editing to us, but I wondered why they were filming me and Jamie on our hands and knees cleaning up the mess. Was America that starved for entertainment?

When we saw the incident in the finished pilot, we couldn't believe what we saw. A second camera had caught the collision. Some Loony Tune sounding music was added in the background while the shot of a dozen eggs hitting the floor played out in slow motion, then a second time, and then in reverse, and then forward again but speeded up this time. Then they showed the two of us on the floor with the mess as the music morphed into "Another One Bites the Dust." I had to admit, it was pretty funny. Everyone in the screening room seemed to be laughing, not just an obligatory laugh, but genuine guffawing.

Eventually the pilot got down to brass tacks. The number of couples had been whittled down to eighteen for the actual show. After the pilot, this number would be cut in half. Then every other week as the remaining couples' back stories unfolded, America would vote for their favorite couple to be the parents of *E-baby*. There were quick interviews given with each couple, some led only by Jenny, some by just Dr. Bauschard, and some where they worked together as a team. Emily Bauschard was already showing some potential as an on-camera personality, something I had suspected she was hoping to prove from the start. It was strange to see these eighteen couples flash by so quickly. Just as soon as you found one couple interesting, they disappeared to make way for the next. We were told from the start that the writers would be going for diversity, and in front of us on that screen was diversity with a capital D. No two couples shared much of a similarity in general appearance, speech, background, or the way they interacted with each other. And they were all childless. The producers were stating the obvious when they told us that anyone who already had a child would automatically be written off by the viewers as undeserving, regardless of their circumstances. Without a doubt, all competing for *E-baby* would have to be in the same childless position.

As the last of the couples finished their back story on why they were adopting, I leaned over Jamie to make a comment to Michael. Glancing at my pad I said, "I really like couples number four and fourteen," I began. "They're funny, maybe just a little off the wall, but they seem like they'd be really good parents."

Before I could continue my analysis, Michael interrupted me. The fact that he didn't even have to look at his reference sheet to know who I was talking about reminded me how good he was at his job. "We figured they'd both score really high, but you'll only see one of them in the mix after the pilot," he said.

"Why is that?" I asked.

"They're both black. We don't really need two black couples, so one of them will have to go."

"But what if they both really deserve to be in the top nine?"

"Not going to happen."

"How do you know?"

Michael's answer took me off guard, but by now, it shouldn't have. "We had the top nine chosen before we even finished shooting the pilot interviews. There's a lot going on that you two haven't even seen. We're looking at where these people live, what they do for a living, and what the dynamics of their families are right now. We have to make sure that when we follow them around at work or at home, it's going to be worthwhile for America to take that journey with us." Suddenly Michael sounded a little more like a salesman than I would have preferred.

I felt myself getting a little red in the face. "I understand the need for the program to stay interesting, but are you telling me that this whole thing is rigged? Please don't tell me you already know who is going to wind up with *E-baby*," I said.

Michael answered, "Of course not. America gets to start voting once we get the number down to nine finalists. Don't worry. I thought by now you trusted me." Michael sounded hurt, and I felt guilty for making the accusation.

"I do trust you," I said. "I'm just new to show biz, I guess."

Jamie was quietly sitting between us in no-comment mode. She was always doodling whenever there was a piece of paper in front of her. The couples guide on her clipboard was covered in pencil sketches of trees and birds and an array of geometric shapes. In one corner was a more legitimate drawing of a young smiling couple that was very lifelike and resembled couple number seven. I wasn't sure if she had drawn it because she was impressed by the couple, or more likely because seven was her lucky number.

Michael retreated to the back of the room to talk to a cluster of production people, and I grabbed the opportunity to get Jamie's take on what had just transpired. "So what do you think?" I asked her. "You're unusually quiet."

She continued retracing some of the shapes she had already drawn. "It doesn't seem like they really care who wins," was all she said.

"I know. But listen to what you just said. You just summed it up. Someone is out to win a baby. It didn't sound so weird when they first proposed this to us, but now that I see all these people's faces...I don't know. It's not like they're trying to be the next *American Idol* or win a pile of money on *Survivor*. These people are going for a baby," I said, sensing Jamie was having the same misgivings as I was.

She stopped her tracing and looked me in the eye. "You just told Michael you trusted him. I think we both need to do that. No one has ever done what we're doing. The reason they think it's going to be such a big deal is because it's groundbreaking. No one has ever adopted a baby on national television before. I figure all of these people have been checked out, and they're all worthy. I think the best thing for us is to not even care who wins because they're all good people."

Leave it to Jamie to put it in perspective. She was right, of course. The best way to approach this was to not get emotionally vested in any of the couples. We needed to look at them as equal, not apples and oranges, but all apples. If television viewers wanted to get wrapped up in the process, let them.

The next day the same group gathered to watch the second episode. It was mostly a recapping of highlights from the pilot. It was clear that Michael and his team had no intention of letting us in on any results in advance. It was apparent from the amount of screen time allotted to certain couples, that they would likely make it into the final nine. The final shot of the show was a montage of the nine finalists getting the news. There was no speaking, just filmed footage accompanied by an instrumental version of Kool and the Gang's "Celebrate." At the end of the montage the music faded out as the image of the last selected couple froze and morphed into a shot of Jenny McCreary leaning against a crib in some perfectly decorated nursery we had never seen before.

Jenny laid out the rules for America, telling them how they would get to follow the lives of these nine couples and get to know them. By the time she was finished speaking, it was easy to see how the carefully constructed script was designed to convince people that being part of something like this was a rare opportunity. The future of a young life was in their hands. Their decision could make or break the dreams of the folks they had just been introduced to. They needed to get to know them, and soon they would have the opportunity to vote every other week to narrow the search for *E-baby's* parents. The timing had been meticulously studied by the writers to make sure that Jamie's official due date in late June coincided closely to the time when America would cast its final votes for the winner. An agreement was already in place with a hospital so that filming on site outside the delivery room was an option. Backup plans, in case there was an earlier-than-expected delivery, were also hammered out.

The real work for us started a week later as we were shuttled every day to a new location to be part of the filming. The pilot and first episode were being perfected through final editing, and the time had come for everyone to start staying a step ahead by gathering footage for the upcoming episodes. To Jamie and me, it seemed like a whirlwind of randomness. We hovered off camera as the nine couples put their lives on display for the world to see. Occasionally, Jamie would be asked to sit in couple number two's kitchen and ask them a question provided by the writers, or be waiting in a driveway to greet couple number eight on their return from a bike ride around their neighborhood. None of it made any sense, but by now I knew that when it was all pieced together, it would magically draw viewers into our lives and the lives of the nine couples.

Time flew by as the filming continued. Six weeks' worth of work provided three more episodes "in the can." Vague ads on ABC throughout the day promised audiences a "truly unique reality show experience that was coming their way just in time for the holidays." As the weeks went by, the ads included glimpses of the footage that had already been shot and edited. The first time Jamie saw one of these ads on television was during a commercial break from *The Middle*.

"Oh, my god!" she shouted. "Look at this. We're on TV!"

The truth was, she was on TV, but I knew she was including me so I wouldn't feel left out.

The commercial for *E-baby* ended with a close-up of Jamie looking almost angelic. She was sitting in a park with children running and playing in the background. Speaking to no one in particular, the music swelled as she said, "I made a baby, and I made a difference."

"When did they film that?" I asked. "I don't remember that park."

"That's because I was never there. I said that corny line in the studio a few weeks ago. I couldn't understand why I was sitting on a park bench on an empty sound stage, but now I know. They put fake kids behind me. Nice touch."

"They're real kids," I said.

"You know what I mean," she countered.

I sensed she was unhappy with what she had just seen so I tried to do some damage control. "You look great," I offered. "And you sound like a professional actress."

"I made a baby, and I made a difference? Did those words actually come out of my mouth? I don't even remember saying that. I sounded like a moron."

"No you didn't. You sounded like a sweet, caring person who is trying to do something good in the world."

"Nice try. I sounded like a moron. My parents are going to disown me," she lamented.

"Well, if that happens, maybe we can put you up for adoption on season two," I said, regretting my words instantly.

"It's not funny. What if everyone hates me for

doing this? I keep getting a weird vibe now when I read my e-mails from everyone back home. I feel like the commercial should have me saying, 'I made a baby, and I sold out.' I can't believe that some mothers' rights groups or religious zealots aren't picketing outside the studio every day."

"The press on *E-baby* has emphasized that we're doing this for a noble cause. You have to get over this," I said.

It's impossible to tell someone how they should think, and I knew I had no right to dictate Jamie's feelings to her. The sudden appearance of random advertising popping up everywhere only magnified her uncertainty about the circus we had started. A few days later when we stopped at a mini-mart to get Jamie a caffeine-free Diet Coke, the pregnant clerk behind the counter was wearing a tee shirt, stretched over her round belly, with 'I made a baby, and I made a difference' emblazoned on it. It was written in the same colorful font as the eBay logo. "Hurry up and pay her," said Jamie. "I think I'm going to puke." By the time I got outside, Jamie was sitting on a bench at a bus stop. The straw protruding from her drink cup was in her mouth, but I could see she was not drinking the Diet Coke.

"You're allowed to drink that," I said. "It's paid for."

"I'm okay," she said as she took a long draw on the straw. "We can't fight it," she said as she pointed to the bus approaching the bench we were sitting on. Advertising for our show took up the entire side of the bus. Written inside a drawing of a playpen were the words, 'Make a difference. Watch *E-baby* on ABC.'

Michael set us up with his business accountant, assuring us that he had done well by him and trusted him implicitly. This financial wizard arranged to make it really easy for us to not be encumbered with the money end of things. Every few days I would check our accounts on line and was stunned by the amount of money that was coming in from our paychecks as consultants, and what was coming from our share of *E-baby* merchandising.

Jamie didn't mind leaving this responsibility to me. One day I saw we had each passed the $200,000 mark. "Guess how much?" I asked her, turning the laptop screen toward her so she could see.

Without looking at it, she said, "I can't imagine. You told me we were making more than I could imagine, so I can't imagine."

"Over two hundred grand...each," I said.

I figured she was going to be alright dealing with her personal demons when she smiled and said, "Let's go buy something really expensive."

CHAPTER TWELVE – "ME AND MRS. JONES"

The episodes with the first four couples to bite the dust were no-brainers to figure out. The Watsons always seemed to have drinks in their hands. They were the first to go. American viewers would never forgive themselves if they handed a baby over to a couple of drunks. What America didn't realize was that the director of *E-baby* was often suggesting the Watsons celebrate something with a drink, or unwind with a beer after work, assuring them that it portrayed a relaxed, casual environment. It was subtle, but the impression was made that the Watsons were probably headed to Betty Ford any day.

The Constantinos were next. I think their appeal at first was that they were interestingly ethnic. As the cameras followed them around at home, they seemed to be a bit too ethnic. Their house was decorated in early American Greek immigrant, reminiscent of the house belonging to the girl's parents from *My Big Fat Greek Wedding*. America was probably already picturing a baby decked out in traditional Greek garb, being forced to dance a Pentozali out in the front yard before going into the house to crack eggs with fifty relatives. I'm sure the Greek demographic all rallied around the phones to vote for the Constantinos, but their efforts fell short of what was needed to keep them in the running.

The Baxters were one of two affluent couples in

the running, and I was not surprised to see them go next. They voiced their great intentions of providing a privileged life for their baby, but by this point in the series, they were coming off as snooty. Nobody wanted to see *E-baby* grow up to be a spoiled brat. Amanda Baxter took America into the room she had set up for the possible new addition to her family. The nursery she created was richly furnished and beautifully decorated. Unfortunately for the Baxters, it also reeked of presumption, as if they deserved America's votes because they had already gone to the trouble of creating such a beautiful space for the baby.

The last of the obvious couples to get the axe were the Nybergs, a highly likable couple who always enjoyed good-natured arguments on camera. They never argued over things of much importance, and for awhile these spats were vastly entertaining. Each week America waited to see what would set one of the Nybergs against the other and how it would be resolved. Around week four the arguing turned, quite simply, annoying. I imagined that America was wondering when these two would ever just shut up and go on with their lives. It was bad enough having to listen to them week after week, so America certainly couldn't bring itself to put a baby into that situation day in and day out.

Jamie and I were at our apartment getting ready to be picked up by a studio driver for our ride to today's filming location. We were headed to a grocery store not too far away from where we lived. Today we were filming some "everyday life" footage of one of the couples, something we were used to by now. It was easier now as the number of couples decreased by one every two weeks. Instead of rushing to get through at least two couples per day, we only had to cover one. This allowed for a more leisurely pace.

I paused at the table near our front door to get the apartment key I always kept in a small dish. I saw Jamie's legal pad and picked it up. "Do you want your pad?" I shouted. It was a rhetorical question; she took the pad with her every day.

We got into the car exchanging pleasantries with Mitchell and headed for our location. The grocery store was in a small strip mall near the highway, and I used the travel time to look over the top page of Jamie's pad. She had organized the five finalists, in no particular order as far as I could tell.

Jones, Derrick & Daleta	*Black - funniest, sincere*
Venucci, Kevin & Faschetti, Dwayne	*Gay - most interesting, witty*
Wygant, Ned & Blossom	*Rich - most stable*
Moreland, Denny & Candace	*Religious - salt of the earth*
Karnes, Adam & Luanne	*Older - hippies, kind*

I nodded in agreement with her brief summary of each couple. She had hit the nail on the head with each of them. I was getting excited to see what today would bring. I was at the point now where I realized it was anybody's game and my knack for being able to tell who would be voted off might be a thing of the past. I did, however, always manage to select my top pick of who would be safe from elimination. I based this on the footage of the couple that stood out as the warmest or had the most feel-good potential.

We met Deleta Jones in the parking lot of the shopping plaza. When we pulled up, she had the window of her car rolled down and was explaining to Michael why her husband Derrick was not with her.

"I told him to get his butt in the car, but he said, 'No way.' I didn't pay attention to what all he ate last night, but he overdid it, and I think it gave him the poops, if you forgive my French," said Deleta. "I figured you'd all be here waiting for me, so I came without him. Trust me, it's better this way. He was in a nasty mood. Serves him right, I say. He was eating like a pig last night. Like a pig!" She laughed and shook her head.

"No, it's all good," said Michael. "It'll change it up a bit. Our most recent shots have been with the two of you together, so this is a fresh approach."

"Why anyone would want to watch me grocery shop is beyond me. But you're the boss. Hey, do you mind if we stop at the Verizon first? My phone has completely gone and quit on me."

"No, of course not. Whatever you want to do," said Michael as he waved the camera guys ahead so they could prep the workers at Verizon and get things ready. Getting waivers and disclaimers signed was a quick formality that was becoming easier each week. *E-baby* had already made a big enough impact on the surrounding community. Everyone from businesses to stores to doctors' offices wanted on the bandwagon to be a part of America's favorite new pastime.

The van crew filmed Deleta pulling up in front of the Verizon store a couple of times. She had learned not to question them and just politely obliged. On the third time parking her car, she hit the cement parking stop, noisily running her front bumper over the top of it. She panicked, threw the car in reverse causing the horrible noise to repeat itself as she backed up. The camera crew was visibly pleased at this minor mishap. Any incident that could be edited to be funny or sad or interesting in any way was a good thing.

Deleta climbed out of her car shaking her head. "If Derrick was here, I would be a dead woman," she declared to no one in particular. She walked to the front of the car, inspected the bumper and realized there was no visible damage. The van crew changed position and took various close-up shots of the bumper.

"Well, what he don't know won't hurt him," Deleta laughed to herself as she entered the store.

A nervous store manager greeted her personally, already coached in how to relax and just behave as naturally as possible.

"Listen, honey, just ignore all these other people here with me, and you're gonna get back to work a lot quicker, I can guarantee that," Deleta said to him. He was a lanky, somewhat nerdy guy, who looked just like the Verizon store managers you saw on Verizon commercials, right down to the gold tag on his lapel that identified him as Tony.

"And how can I help you today, Mrs. Jones?" inquired Tony, trying to sound as natural as possible.

"I need a new one of these," Deleta replied, as she handed over her cell phone to the manager. Tony immediately popped the protective back off the phone and examined it as Deleta continued speaking. "It's a few months old, so maybe you don't have one just exactly like it…"

"You got this wet," interrupted Tony.

"You said what?" asked Deleta.

Tony looked nervous but continued. "I said, 'You got this wet.' Do you see this red dot on the inside of the phone? This means you got the phone wet."

Deleta frowned and looked at Tony as if he had just accused her of drowning a kitten.

After an awkward silence, Tony asked Deleta, "Mrs. Jones, did you get your phone wet?"

"Well, I might have set my drink on it, but I didn't spill it," she replied indignantly.

"Nonetheless, I can't give you a new phone if your dot is red," explained Tony.

"Quit talking about my red dot. I don't know anything about my damn dot turning red, and I never asked you to give me anything. I'll pay for the new phone."

"I'm sorry," Tony assured her. "I wasn't accusing you of anything. I know we don't have this exact phone in stock anymore, but I have one that's very similar. I'll be back with it in just a second." Tony beat a quick retreat into the nearby stock room to look for the replacement phone.

Deleta glanced at a sales girl standing off to the side. "Did you hear me ask for a free phone? I didn't ask for a free phone. You better believe I'm checking the dot on that new phone before I leave here," declared Deleta.

Tony was back with the new phone. "Here we are," he said cheerfully.

"Before you even take that thing out of the box, tell me one thing. Do I get my dip dip?" asked Deleta.

"I'm sorry," said Tony. "Your what?"

"My dip dip."

"Well, I don't know," replied Tony cautiously, as if he were afraid of being lured into some kind of trap.

"Tony," Deleta began in a calm soothing voice. "Do you do this for a living?"

"Yes, ma'am."

"So, you sell phones for a living. And you can't even tell me if I get my dip dip on this phone?"

"I...I," Tony stammered. "I'm not really sure what your dip dip is."

Deleta rolled her eyes. "My dip dip. My Intranet."

I knew I was watching the kind of thing that would make great reality television. This woman was a riot in front of the camera, and something inside me was telling me she had what it took to be a great mother as well. Her good nature and warmth shone through in every word and action, even when she was exasperated with a Verizon clerk.

"Oh, yes, of course. Your Internet is on this phone, just like your old one. It'll just take me a minute to transfer all the information from the memory card on your old one," Tony said.

"Then I am one happy woman, and when you ring me up, I will be one happy woman on her way," Deleta said with a smile.

She exited the store with her new phone dangling from her wrist in its plastic Verizon bag. She stopped abruptly in front of her car and turned around, almost causing a pile-up with the crew trailing behind her. She stood on her tiptoes, looked over their heads and spotted Michael toward the back of the entourage walking next to Jamie and me.

Deleta shouted to him, "Hey, is it okay if we just walk down two doors to the PetSmart? Rocky needs a new flea collar." Rocky was her Jack Russell terrier. I thought of Rocky as Derrick and Deleta's trump card. Watching the way they doted on the little dog was heartwarming. When you saw the love and attention he got, you couldn't help but make the connection between their pet and what a child might expect from them.

"Rocky. Sure!" shouted Michael, as Deleta disappeared through the sliding electronic glass door.

While Deleta searched for the flea collar, Jamie and I accompanied Michael and some assistants to the front registers to take care of the obligatory paperwork. Assuming everything would go smoothly, the camera guys followed Deleta and discreetly got footage of her combing the shelves.

While waiting for the manager Michael mumbled something about not having to wait around if he had known in advance that these were the stops Deleta had wanted to make.

"But I thought it was this kind of spontaneity that you liked," I said. "Besides, Deleta is a riot."

"She shouldn't be drawing a box around the dog," he said. "It's kind of a high strung animal."

"Are you serious?" I asked. "You think the fact they have a dog is going to negatively impact how they're perceived?"

"Absolutely," Michael said confidently. "It was a point of consideration from the very beginning. We figured to make it fair, every couple had to be childless. For a while, we thought of not letting any finalists in who had pets. No matter how crazy you think it might sound, I'm pretty certain the Joneses are going to lose this because of that dog."

"That's where we disagree. I think it puts them out front. Surely you've seen how much they love that dog. They've had that dog with them in almost every shot."

"Exactly. Big mistake on their part. They already have something to love. Subconsciously that's how the viewers will see it. The dog is going to cost them."

I knew I was just going to add to Michael's frustration with my naivety, but I said it anyway. "That's not right."

The store manager approached us, and in a few minutes the paperwork was taken care of. Deleta, with the crew in tow, eventually appeared at the counter and set a small square box down in front of a young man, a clerk who had excitedly volunteered to be on camera to wait on Mrs. Jones.

"Is that all?" he inquired.

"That'll do it, honey," replied Deleta.

On the wall behind the cash register was a sign taped above a folding table. On the table was a picnic basket half filled with cans of pet food. Prominently highlighted with fluorescent marker on the sign were the words 'SHELTER DONATIONS'. Underneath these words, taped-up photocopies of pets from the L.A. Animal Shelter were displayed in order to tug at the heartstrings of customers. Deleta was digging through her purse and apparently hadn't noticed the sign.

"Would you like to feed a kitty?" the clerk cheerfully inquired.

"What kitty? Where's the kitty?" Deleta asked as she glanced around the store and then down near her feet, obviously expecting to see a hungry kitten nearby who needed to be fed.

"The kitty isn't here," explained the young man. "The kitty is at the animal shelter."

"Oh, I don't have time to go to no shelter. I've got all these people with me and they need to film me shopping," said Deleta.

"You don't have to actually go to the shelter," he said.

Deleta interrupted him. "Well, if the kitty ain't here, and I'm not going to the shelter, how am I gonna feed the kitty?" she asked.

"Let me explain," he offered nervously, afraid he was going to dig a hole he couldn't get out of before Deleta buried him in it. "You give me a dollar. I let you pick a can of cat food out of one of these bags.

Then we put the cat food in the picnic basket there," he said, indicating the table behind him, "and when the basket is full, we take it to the shelter."

Deleta stared at the clerk like this was maybe the craziest thing she had ever heard. After a beat she smiled and said, "Okay. That sounds good. I'm gonna feed the kitty!"

The clerk indicated some paper bags filled with cans of cat food on the counter next to the cash register. Deleta reached into the closest bag and pulled out a tiny can of Fancy Feast. She rocked forward on her toes and leaned on the counter to get a better look at the table behind the clerk. She had a puzzled look on her face as she noticed some of the bigger cans that had already found their way into the basket.

"This little can is a dollar?" she asked with disbelief in her voice. "This teeny little can costs a dollar?"

"Well," the clerk said smiling, "if you want to put it back and pick a different one, I won't tell."

"Oh no. This is fine. All I can say is that kitty's eatin' better than me."

I glanced at the customers and the film crew standing close by and noticed the giant smiles plastered on their faces. I was convinced that this woman was going to charm the television audience, just as she had charmed everyone standing there right now.

The rest of the week was spent following each of the other four couples: one to church, one to work, one to a meeting for volunteers for a neighborhood cleanup project, and one to a family picnic. There were moments with each one that merited being shown as part of the show, but I was convinced that Derrick and Deleta were safe thanks to the cell phone and flea collar shopping trip.

Michael had made me second guess myself. When it was time to watch the episode I found myself feeling nervous. Jamie and I had decided to wait to watch each post-edit episode on television at its 8 P.M. time slot, in order to see it as everyone else in the country was seeing it.

The music behind the bumper scraping footage was ominous. It made Deleta's funny comment about being a dead woman sound as if she was serious. The footage of her asking Verizon Tony, "You said what?" was repeated from the camera two angle. The first time it played, it sounded funny. The second time made her sound pushy.

"Wait a minute," said Jamie. "She only said that once. They pulled some tricky editing there."

We continued to watch the rest of the show without making any more comments. I was waiting for my favorite part, never thinking for a second that I wouldn't get to see it. When the production and editing teams omitted the part of the PetSmart trip where Deleta gave the clerk a big bear hug before leaving the store, I knew where this was headed. The last part of the Jones' portion of the show showed Rocky barking and jumping against the front door of the Jones' house upon Deleta's return from shopping. A week later, Deleta was holding Rocky in her arms, seated next to her husband Derrick, when Jenny McCreary broke the news to them that America had voted and, sadly, they were eliminated from *E-baby*.

CHAPTER THIRTEEN – "THE ANNIVERSARY BRUNCH"

Being gay, Kevin Venucci and Dwayne Faschetti were the wild card couple, at least in my opinion. However, the word on the street from ABC's research department showed that there was barely a ripple when their inclusion as one of the final eighteen *E-baby* contestant couples was announced. The show's focus for them this week was an easy call. Kevin and Dwayne were celebrating their second wedding anniversary with a Sunday brunch, and Michael, Lili, Jamie, and I were invited to join the other guests that included about two dozen relatives and close friends of theirs. It was going to be at Cucinas, a trendy restaurant in the valley that had a private dining room large enough to be conducive to filming. I had a feeling that ABC was footing the bill for this lavish shindig, but I didn't really care one way or the other. As Jamie pointed out, a free meal was a free meal.

I admired the courage that Kevin and Dwayne had shown from the very beginning of the show. I figured it probably wasn't going to be easy for them to put their life together as a couple on television for the world to see. On the other hand, television is exactly where gay couples were becoming more and more acceptable to everyone, including Middle America. Just about every television show now had a gay character or even a gay couple as leading characters.

It made me think of how much satisfaction Ellen DeGeneres must have felt after having her sitcom cancelled way back in the day when her character first came out on her TV series, and now here she was today, dominating the daytime talk show battle. If someone had told me, even just five years ago, that a lesbian in her fifties would someday be a spokes model for Cover Girl, I would have called him delusional. The business world never even raised an eyebrow when Ron Johnson took over as CEO of JCPenney, immediately revamped the store's basic structure, and stuck Ellen out in front of it as its new spokesperson.

Ellen had featured Kevin and Dwayne on her talk show back when they were first selected for *E-baby*. I thought it would give them unfair exposure, an advantage over the other couples, but Michael assured me that permission was enthusiastically granted by ABC for their appearance. Any publicity for the show was good publicity. My first impression of them was favorable. They were clean cut, polite professionals who had responded to the ad for adoptive parents, motivated in exactly the same way as the straight couples. Their "lifestyle" may have been different from the others, but the bottom line was simply that they wanted to have a baby. Gay adoption was becoming commonplace, but being selected for *E-baby* automatically put two handsome faces out there as spokesmen for this issue. They informed Ellen that they were only one of more than a hundred gay, married couples who had signed up to vie for a spot when *E-baby* was just getting off the ground.

Kevin worked in city planning for Orange County. He was more of a stereotypical businessman than a stereotypical gay man. He appeared everywhere in a dark colored suit which was always accompanied by the perfect shoes and the perfect tie. He wore wire-rimmed glasses, and the only accessories he sported were tasteful cuff links. His voice conveyed self-assurance and, well, masculinity.

Dwayne was pretty much the opposite. He worked as a loan officer in a bank. Like Kevin, he looked the professional at work, but didn't wear his work clothes as comfortably. As soon as he would get home, he would head immediately to the bedroom and emerge twenty minutes later in the beach apparel he favored. Typically this included cargo shorts, a flowery Hawaiian shirt, and brightly striped flip flops. The first time filming was done at their house, Michael suggested that Kevin change into something more relaxed.

"No, this is fine," said Kevin.

"It's just that you look like one of you is headed for the opera and the other one is headed for a luau," explained Michael.

It was obvious Dwayne had no intention of changing. He was too busy moving magazines to different edges of the coffee table in the living room, wanting them to look just right for the cameras. Kevin disappeared for a few minutes and emerged pretty much the same as when he had left the room. The jacket of his suit had been replaced with a cashmere sweater, but he was still wearing the same tie and shoes.

"There, that's better," he announced as he came in and pulled Dwayne down next to him as he sat on the sofa. He said it with such a tone of finality that suggesting any other change to his wardrobe didn't seem like an option.

The first on-camera interview with them consisted of them talking about their work and their hobbies. Kevin was obviously passionate about city planning, everything from beautification projects to housing for low-income families. Dwayne was passionate about bike riding and gardening. Kevin enjoyed a good discussion about the National Endowment of the Arts, while Dwayne enjoyed a good discussion about the natural endowment of Chippendale dancers. I was wondering why the gay issue was never addressed by Jenny McCreary until I realized that it was completely unnecessary. It was hard to forget what separated this couple from the others every time Dwayne opened his mouth to speak.

When Jamie and I arrived at Cucina's on the day of the anniversary brunch, Michael and Lili were already inside seeing to the details of the filming. The tables had been moved into an odd configuration, but one that made it more conducive for the cameras to catch conversations and reactions.

The original idea was to mix the Venucci's in with the Faschetti's to create one big, happy, blended family, but obviously whoever came up with that idea wasn't Italian. Although there was much hugging and kissing when the two families greeted each other, when it came time to be seated, everyone wanted to be sitting at their assigned tables with familia. Venuccis with Venuccis, Faschettis with Faschettis. Once everyone was seated, Michael did his usual "meet and greet" with the guests who had never gone through the experience of being on-camera. He explained to them the importance of acting natural and ignoring the camera.

It had been determined ahead of time that Kevin and Dwayne would have certain topics to stick to at dinner. There was also a list carried by each of the crew members with "Highlighted Events" printed at the top. The goal was to get enough footage through these special moments in order to convey Kevin and Dwayne's "story" to America. The list had only five items.

1) welcoming (friends and relatives)
2) dinner conversation (focus on K.'s and D.'s families)
3) the toast
4) the cake (dessert)
5) departure

My neck was strained from tilting my head to read Cameraman Two's list. As I finished reading, Michael instructed the half of the room closest to the door to re-enter so that they could be "met" on camera. Kevin and Dwayne were each given a Mimosa as a prop to hold while they greeted guests at the door. This was not a good idea. Dwayne, nervous as a tick, found the glass awkward since he insisted on hugging absolutely everyone who entered the room. He downed his drink after the first hug, and immediately a waitress with a tray of Mimosas handed him another one. Item one from the list took about a half hour to complete, and in that time Dwayne had four Mimosas.

As soon as everyone was seated, Father McGuire, a priest seated at the head table, stood to give the prayer before the meal commenced.

"Where did you find him?" I whispered to Michael.

"He's the guy who married them," Michael answered. "I flew him in all the way from Massachusetts. They got married in Boston."

"Nice touch," I said.

Halfway through the prayer thanking God for bringing these friends and families together on this special day, Dwayne seemed to forget that the good father was in the middle of a prayer. "God, this smells good. I'm starving!" exclaimed Dwayne. There was an awkward pause, and then Father McGuire continued his prayer as if nothing had happened.

"Sorry!" interrupted Dwayne, moments later in a loud stage whisper.

Jamie bowed her head, but it wasn't in prayer. She had started to laugh and that got Lili started. I'm sure some of the guests might have suspected that Michael Olsen would have the priest back up and start the prayer again, but I knew better. Michael was smiling, but I knew it was because he saw something happening that would make good television. I glanced at the head table and saw Kevin staring at Dwayne, the look on his face somewhere between anger and embarrassment. Dwayne had moved on to straight champagne now and was holding a full flute in front of his face. I realized he was squinting and looking through the glass to watch Father McGuire finish the blessing.

The prayer ended, and after a plate of food was placed in front of each guest, two cameras hovered around the head table while a third traveled around the room, randomly eavesdropping on the guests as they commented on the happy couple and their desire to adopt a baby. If they thought they'd wind up on national television, I had a feeling that most of them were going to be disappointed. I suspected the antics at the head table were going to provide more than enough for an engrossing episode of *E-baby*.

At our small round table, the four of us barely spoke a word as we tried to hear everything that was happening next door to us. Kevin was doing his best to lead the conversation with enough dignity to counter the slurry speech that was coming from Dwayne. Kevin's grandmother, Lydia Venucci, asked a pertinent question that caused both hand-held cameras to swing in her direction.

"Kevin, dear," she began. "I think I speak for everyone in the family when I say we have finally accepted the idea of you two becoming parents, but do you really think that this is the way to go?"

"And what way is that, Grandmother?" replied Kevin.

"On the television. I think family things should be

more private. But what do I know? I'm a thousand years old!"

"We're doing this because we want to start a family more than anything in the world," said Kevin. Dwayne's eyes immediately welled up with tears, and he reached for Kevin's hand, knocking a coffee cup off its saucer in the process.

"It's true. More than anything in the world," echoed Dwayne.

It was obvious that Kevin's grandmother was not going to be dissuaded from getting down to the nitty gritty. "Don't you think that people probably won't, oh, how do I say this so you don't get offended..." she began. It didn't matter, since everyone at the table knew exactly where she was headed.

"You can say it, Grandmother. You don't think people will vote to give a baby to the gay couple," Kevin said matter of factly. "You know, times and attitudes have changed, even in the last year. I'm pretty sure that people will relate to what Hillary Clinton said. It takes a village. Now I know that's just a broad generalization, but I think the whole country has been made aware that the family unit doesn't have to mean a traditional mother and father."

Dwayne chimed in, "Yeah, Hillary didn't say the village had to have vaginas in it. It's..." The horrified look Kevin shot him stopped him mid sentence. "...just a village," he finished.

After signaling to the closest cameraman to move away, Kevin turned in his chair to face Dwayne. "Dwayne," he said quietly, "I'd like you to go to the men's room and throw some cold water on your face. You look a little flushed. I'm going to have a nice cup of coffee waiting here for you when you get back. Okay?"

Dwayne did as he was told and the head table began discussing more mundane topics. After complimenting the restaurant on how nicely appointed the room was for the brunch, they moved on to the weather and how the trend of higher temperatures across the country was affecting everything from housing sales to the price of carrots. Kevin tipped back in his chair and steadied himself by grasping the back of mine.

"Would you do me a favor?" he asked.

"Sure." I wondered why he wasn't hitting Michael up for the favor. Michael was more in charge of the proceedings than I was, but I guess Kevin was just going with the nearest person.

"Would you check on Dwayne? I want to make sure he's okay, but I think I should stay here with the family."

"No problem. I'd be glad to," I assured him. I excused myself reluctantly, not wanting to miss whatever might be coming next at the table beside ours.

"Tell me every word I miss," I whispered to Jamie through closed teeth like a ventriloquist.

I made my way to the men's room. When I pushed the door open and walked in, I thought at first it was empty. Just as I turned to leave I heard a sniffle coming from around the corner near the sinks.

Leaning against the wall next to the hand dryers was Dwayne, patting his eyes with a handful of Kleenexes he had pulled from a box on the sink.

"I'm screwing it up," he said. "I just get so nervous. I can tell that Kevin wants to kill me right now. Why would I say 'vagina' in front of a camera? That's not even it! Why would I say 'vagina' in front of our relatives? I can't go back out there."

"It'll be all right," I said, attempting to comfort him. "You have to get back out there, though. I'm afraid that door is going to open any second and one of those cameras is going to come barging in here."

"No, you don't understand. I'm always messing things up, and then Kevin winds up having to save me. When I had only been working at the bank for a couple of weeks, a co-worker told me that the employees decided that lunch on the next Friday was going to be a Share Day. Leave it to me, I volunteered to bring in a CD player to the lunch room. I even said I'd bring in a DVD of *Moonstruck* and we could let it play during lunch."

"Oh, I get it," I said. "You thought Share Day meant..."

"Exactly. Kevin thought it was funny. Once again he managed to keep me from embarrassing myself, and he sent me to work with a bowl of homemade macaroni salad instead. Sometimes I wonder why he'd want to be stuck with someone who can be such an idiot."

"Hey, it was an honest mistake. My impression is you guys make a good team. You're a good match."

"You know, this is the first time I've ever gotten to say a word to you without a dozen people around. You and Jamie must be hoping right now that we get voted out of the running. I wouldn't blame you." Dwayne walked to the mirror and started readjusting his tie and brushing some non-existent lint from the sleeves of his suit jacket. "As soon as I get dressed in a suit I feel and act like a different person. It just isn't me. I wish we hadn't decided to do this whole brunch thing on camera. Kevin thought it would be a good idea. He thought people who watched the show would like to see us mixed in with our combined families, like that would make us seem like a regular couple. He didn't count on me sounding like an idiot. I swear it's not the champagne, it's nerves."

"Then I say you take a deep breath, get over the nerves, and go out there and show everyone what a great dad you'd be." I patted him on the shoulder and made my way to the door.

"Kevin and I would both be good dads, you know. I think people imagine I want to be some kind of mom because on the show I said I'd give up my job for awhile to stay home with the baby. What they don't know is that we decided to go that way because Kevin makes four times what I make." Dwayne looked at me, and I could tell there was something else he was trying to say.

"What is it?" I asked.

"I want to ask you something, but I don't want you to take it the wrong way or be offended," said Dwayne.

"Go ahead."

"Why are you doing this? I've heard the whole explanation, the way the show recaps it every week during the opening credits. But I still have a hard time understanding. Kevin and I want this baby so much. I guess I just can't imagine anyone giving away something I want so badly. Please don't think I'm judging you. I just know I couldn't do it. If by some miracle we end up with *E-baby*, I'll be thanking you but never judging you."

I didn't answer Dwayne's question. "I'll see you out there," I said, and I went back to take my place next to Jamie. After I sat down, Kevin glanced at me nervously. I smiled and gave him a thumbs up.

"What did I miss?" I asked.

"Oh, my God, Kevin's grandmother is relentless," said Jamie. "She's done this complete change of direction and now is insisting they're going to be the last remaining couple. How's Dwayne?"

"Embarrassed. I think he'll be fine. He's determined to come back out here and make a good impression," I added and noted a coffee decanter on the head table, just to the top right corner of Dwayne's place setting.

I could hear Kevin's grandmother, and she was on a roll. "When I see the other three couples you're still up against, I'd have to put you at the top right now," she said wagging her finger in Kevin's direction. "The one couple is a little too obsessed with religion. That can be a turnoff. The other couple seems too old, and they live like hippies. The last ones have money, but money can be a curse. It can't buy everything. It can't buy happiness. But I think the money is just about the only thing they bring to the table."

"I appreciate your confidence, Grandmother," said Kevin, "but you put us on top because you're my grandma and you love us. I'm afraid the rest of the country sees us at the bottom because we're the obvious long shot."

Suddenly Dwayne walked into the room with renewed confidence. He crossed to his chair and before he even sat, he poured a cup of coffee and took a sip. "Sorry. I guess the excitement of the party made me a little crazy there for a minute. What's everyone talking about now?" he asked.

Kevin's grandmother smiled and replied, "Well, dear, I certainly don't think he can be right, but Kevin insists that you're on the bottom."

For a moment I thought Dwayne was going to lose his balance.

"What?" he shrieked.

"Oh, my God, sit down, Dwayne," demanded Kevin.

"I get sent from the room for saying 'vagina' and then you go and tell the entire table…"

"…That we're on the bottom of the remaining couples on *E-baby*," Kevin said, quickly finishing Dwayne's sentence for him. "And isn't that the kind of support we were hoping for? Uncle Ted, Aunt Judy, Grandmother, I hope you're right. But we'll know soon enough. When the hell are we going to have cake?"

I remembered the Highlighted Events list and wondered if the toast was going to get skipped. I guess the list didn't really matter much any more because from that point on Kevin ran the show. Even though the entire room was barely halfway through their food, Kevin marched Dwayne over to the cake table in a corner of the room and got everyone's attention. "On this beautiful Sunday morning, I just want to thank our friends and family for joining us on this special occasion." Kevin began furiously cutting cake and placing pieces on dessert plates. A waitress came over to assist him. He turned to her and curtly said, "I've got it. Thank you." She began loading up a tray with plates of cake and began distributing them. Dwayne stood beside the cake table with a glazed look in his eyes and a fake smile that revealed every tooth.

I really liked Kevin and Dwayne, and right now I felt sorry for them. I also felt guilty when it occurred to me that if it hadn't been for *E-baby*, this probably would have been a really nice anniversary brunch.

CHAPTER FOURTEEN – "THE CHURCH LADY"

Jamie felt uncomfortable whenever she was at the Moreland's for filming. This was the couple she had defined as the religious one. She didn't label them as such in a negative way. She didn't mind going to church. As a matter of fact, she was pretty good about getting Darrell and Vincent to church, at least until they were teenagers when their attendance and interest dwindled. She was raised Catholic but somehow had wound up attending a Lutheran church in Slippery Rock when she went away to school the first time, mostly because the Lutheran Church was in walking distance from where she lived. She liked it and stuck with it when she moved to Edinboro and then Erie. Her mother was disappointed that Jamie hadn't maintained her ties to Catholicism. She didn't seem comforted by Jamie's observation that Lutheran was just about the same as Catholic, but with the bingo sucked out of it.

It didn't take much to push Jamie's off button though. She had tried attending a Lutheran church after our first few weeks in California. She came back to the apartment after the service one morning and was fuming. A very enthusiastic woman had greeted her and welcomed her to the church as Jamie was passing through the narthex on her way out.

"Thanks for coming," she said. "We love seeing

new faces here at St. John's."

"You have a beautiful church," said Jamie. "It reminds me of home."

"And where would that be, Ms. LaRusso?" She had read Jamie's name from the "Hello, My Name Is" name tag that had been handed to Jamie when she entered the church.

"I'm from Pennsylvania," Jamie answered. She was determined to avoid going into the circumstances that had brought her to California.

"Oh, really?" responded the woman with a slight frown. "It's just that I noticed you took communion."

"Oh, I'm sorry. The minister invited all who believed to come to the altar to receive the body and blood of Jesus." Jamie had an instinctive defensiveness. "Was I not supposed to join in?" She thought maybe she wasn't supposed to participate in communion unless she was a member of that particular church.

"Oh, no. I guess it's alright. It's just that it didn't count," the woman said.

"Excuse me?"

The woman explained. "Your church in Pennsylvania is in a different synod, so your communion here wouldn't really count."

"Wouldn't really count?" Jamie felt her face flush at the woman's condescending tone. "Wouldn't really count for whom?"

"For you. You're a member of the Pennsylvania / West Virginia Synod so your communion here doesn't really count. But I guess there's no harm done. It just doesn't count."

Two things flashed through Jamie's mind. One, this woman really knew a lot about the way the Lutheran Church in America was structured. And two, she was a horse's ass.

"Wouldn't communion be between me and God?" Jamie asked.

"No, not if you're not in your home synod. But thanks for coming. It was lovely to meet you."

If Jamie hadn't had that conversation, she probably would have had a little more patience with Candace Moreland. Candace was a bit overzealous in the religion department. She tied her every move, every decision, to what Jesus would do or what Jesus would think about it. We were both quite surprised that the Morelands had made it this far on *E-baby*, but as Michael pointed out with his infallible programming wisdom, it was a reflection on the times. There were so many dangers today that threatened the safety and welfare of kids everywhere. The ominous threat of violence had left the city and had settled down in the suburbs. This couple, seemingly defined by their zest for religion, assured viewers that this baby would have a safe home, a home protected by God.

Jamie was not totally convinced. "I'm just surprised that people don't see Candace the way I do. It's hard to explain. It's like she uses her religion as some kind of umbrella over her life. And there's this purveying sense of superiority that goes hand in hand with that."

"That's where Denny fits in," Michael said. "He's the ultimate "regular guy". This guy is off the charts when it comes to an audience being able to identify with him. Candace is the shepherd, and Denny is a sheep. And if he's willing to follow her, then it's probably alright for them too."

"Where I come from, we'd call him a wuss," said Jamie.

"Nope. They see him as the ultimate nice guy who provides for his family. He's a stable caregiver with a strong wife, a wife who has a direct line to the Lord. The bottom line is he keeps it real. Women out in TV land love this woman's assertiveness and especially love the fact that her husband follows her lead in everything. Our research tells us that the women voting for *E-baby* far outnumber the men." Once again, Michael put things in perspective. He never stopped demonstrating his ability to analyze what America wanted to see on their televisions.

Candace and Denny had a lovely home. At Candace's suggestion, the filming this week began in the small but tasteful library off the living room of their house. It conveyed warmth and security but didn't appear to be too ostentatious. It was much like the Morelands.

Jenny McCreary nodded to the cameraman who gave her the signal that they were rolling. Candace and Denny were seated side by side on a love seat that had been moved to the center of the room. Jamie was in a wing chair placed at a slight angle to their left. I was the other bookend in an identical wing chair to their right.

Jenny began. "So we're down to the wire, so to speak. Are you surprised to be sitting here right now?"

I noticed that Denny didn't even show the slightest intention of answering, even though the question was thrown in his direction as much as Candace's. He would follow Candace's lead as usual.

"Well, of course we couldn't be more elated that we're still here. Those nice gentlemen looked so brave when they heard that they were voted off last week. I asked the Lord to look after them, even though they're sinners in His eyes, and get them through what has to be a difficult time for them." Denny nodded in agreement. So much for the gay vote.

"So I hear we're in for a real treat this week," Jenny said, making her best effort to gloss over Candace's well intended but politically incorrect remark. "Something about you doing some lay ministry at your church?"

"Well, that would be my little mission, but Denny will be right there to support my efforts to spread some of the Good News. Won't you, honey?" It was somewhat a rhetorical question, so Denny didn't think a verbal response was necessary. He nodded, but Candace was too focused on facing the camera to notice. "Isn't that right?" she prompted.

"Of course," replied Denny. "She's a good little speaker. She filled in for Reverend Pfister one week last summer when he was on vacation. Folks are still telling her how inspiring they thought her sermon was."

"I wasn't used to being anything more than a lay reader every once in a while. But I felt it was an honor to step up to the pulpit when Reverend Pfister called on me to speak the Word in his place," Candace said proudly.

The truth was Michael had tried to talk the Morelands out of Candace's suggestion that their focus this week would involve her latest moment in the spotlight in church. I suspect his reasoning was that anything happening in church would be too solemn or boring to be of much interest to anyone. They came to a compromise, arranging to capture several activities on film. With only three couples to follow this week, there was extra time to devote to each one. The filming of a pinochle game with the Morelands and their neighbors, the Hedlunds, gave Michael a new definition of boring. There wasn't a whiff of controversy. There were no overplayed hands, not even a bidding war for calling trump to provide even a speck of interest. An antiquing trip provided little of anything except for a moment when an antique crib caught Candace's eye. In an uncharacteristic move on Denny's part, he put his foot down and scolded Candace for jumping the gun when she suggested they buy it. Michael and Jamie were huddled off camera commiserating about how dull this venture had turned out to be.

"At least he stood up to her and said no," noted Jamie.

"Over a baby crib. Big deal," said Michael

shaking his head. "This is the point where the excitement and anticipation of the show should be getting everyone in the country worked up and gathered around water coolers debating which couple was going to wind up with *E-baby*. I never wanted a couple to get voted off for being too boring. This is not good."

"Maybe Candace will invoke a miracle when she preaches on Sunday," I offered. "Maybe she'll speak in tongues, or heal a cripple, or talk to a burning bush. That'll give you ratings."

Michael ignored me and continued. "At least we got some decent footage this week with the Karnes and the Wygants." Yesterday the Karnes had elected to be filmed at Disneyland with their niece and nephew. The day before, the Wygants had us follow them to a dedication ceremony for the new lobby of a library. They had made a sizable donation and were asked to be on hand for the official unveiling of the new space. Both couples came off in a positive light. The Karnes were the oldest couple in the running, but they kept up with the niece and nephew effortlessly. It was a good decision on their part, showing the viewers how well they managed a day in an amusement park showing two little kids a good time. When the Wygants were at the library opening, Michael had suggested that Blossom read to some school children who were attending the opening. The library had displayed the kids' drawings and paintings from art class around the new lobby, giving it a warm feeling. Part of the footage showed a cluster of second graders leading Ned and Blossom Wygant around the lobby pointing out which of the works of art they were responsible for. Ned and Blossom made a fuss over each one of them, and the camera showed the reaction of each child as his work was praised. At the time I thought it was a little schmaltzy, but I knew that by the time editing worked their magic, the segment would have the potential to stir up a lot of emotion in the viewers. The last shot was the "money shot." When the time came for Blossom to read to the children, she was seated in a simple folding chair near a display of Dr. Seuss books. Kids were placed around her to frame the picture Michael was trying to portray. Older ones stood behind her while the younger ones were seated on the floor. As Blossom turned the last page of *Horton Hears a Who*, the camera widened the shot a bit and panned slightly to her right, just enough to catch the image of a little girl who had rested her head against Blossom's leg, almost in her lap. There was something very maternal about the image, and I had thought at the time that Michael himself was an artist of sorts.

My instincts told me Michael was between a rock and a hard place. To me it was obvious he had no affinity for the Morelands. If he left them to their own boring devices, they would wind up doing themselves in, and he could have the showdown between the two couples he obviously favored. However, this would be at the cost of viewers having to endure almost thirty-five minutes of snore-worthy programming. But the possibility of television watchers grabbing their remotes to escape from the Morelands was a prospect that Michael couldn't bear.

"So you think she might talk in tongues?" Michael asked me. I knew he was joking, yet I detected some glimmer of hope in his voice that something would shake up the church service.

Candace didn't speak in tongues on Sunday, but boy, did she speak. She rambled on like she was on a mission from God, not only to present a life lesson through her sermon, but to educate the congregation on the entire Old Testament. She veered from imploring them to help their fellow man to explaining in detail the significance of the story of the loaves and fishes. She wove this delivery pattern back and forth. Her sermon had almost reached the half hour mark when I realized I wasn't the only one whose thoughts were drifting. I glanced around the pews and saw that most of the congregation members' eyes had glazed over. Some were politely pretending to be reading out of hymnals or their church bulletins to mask the fact that their eyes were slammed completely shut. Jamie was staring at the ceiling. I suspected she had finished counting the number of candles burning in the many candelabras on the altar and had moved on to counting the panes of glass in the stained glass windows. Michael looked like he was trapped in hell. Even the cameramen were finding it difficult not to fidget. They had stopped moving around the sanctuary to change angles, and all three of them had taken to leaning against the nearest wall or pillar for support. Michael had thought of this possibly happening and had appealed to us to try to stay focused and at least make an effort to look interested. There would be a good chance at any given moment that we'd be on film. I glanced over at Denny who was seated in the pew in front of ours. He was about four feet to the left of us so I had a good view of his profile. I noticed his jaw looked locked. Was he gritting his teeth? His eyes seemed to be burning right into Candace as she was droning on about Lot's wife. I nudged Michael, smiled at him, and made the slightest gesture with my finger to indicate I wanted him to look at Denny. He proceeded to stare at Denny as if he was trying to read his mind.

Candace's voice rose in both volume and pitch. Either she was suddenly re-inspired or she had finally noticed that most of her flock was nodding off. "My friends tell me they have troubles. We all have troubles. They tell me they worry so much they can't sleep at night. I tell them, 'Don't count sheep! Talk to the shepherd!' That's what I tell them!" Denny exhaled and his lips made a motorboat 'bbbrrrhhhbbb' sound that was barely audible. I imagined he had been listening to Candace's chapel-spun advice for many years now. Michael subtly leaned back in the pew, raised his arm up, and placed it behind me in an effort to get Cameraman Three's attention. He pointed his finger and flicked his wrist a few times in Denny's direction while he mouthed the words 'Mr. Moreland.' The cameraman slowly obeyed and inched his way up the aisle staying unobtrusively close to the wall.

Despite having already covered the highlights of Genesis through Numbers, something compelled Candace to return to the Nativity story for some reason. The fact that it was May made this visit to Christmas all the more annoying. This is the sermon that's reserved for Christmas Eve when the candles are lit, the church is glowing, and everyone is waiting to sing "Silent Night". Candace was determined to cover it all, though, and she crossed from behind the pulpit, arms authoritatively akimbo.

"What's the greatest night in the history of mankind?" she asked. There was no response so she answered her own question. "Christmas Eve," she said. She glanced over to an usher who had been standing near the rear entrance of the sacristy. With a flat palm he manipulated four light dimmers at once so the lights faded almost completely. There was still ample light coming through the windows, but Candace's prearranged special lighting effect at least took the glare off the altar and her white robe. It also made the pew area darker, affording much of the congregation better sleeping conditions.

"I want all the people sitting in this church to close their eyes," began Candace as she crossed back to her spot behind the pulpit. That was an easy one. She was actually granting permission for the die-hards who had managed to stay coherent to shut their eyes. "Pretend you are standing outside a humble stable in Bethlehem on that night so many years ago. Go on. Close your eyes. Now, I want you to imagine stepping into that lowly stable. Go ahead. Still keep your eyes

184

closed," instructed Candace. I did a quick side-to-side glance and noted that everyone was in compliance.

"Now take a deep breath. Do you smell that? That's the hay. That strong, earthy smell is the wonderful hay that the animals will be eating for their simple dinner. Everyone, smell it. Go on."

I glanced around again and saw the entire congregation draw a deep breath in unison. It was like watching a mass-hypnotist at work, getting everyone to obey her orders on command without any resistance. I shut my eyes and inhaled quickly through my nose to catch up with the rest of the congregation.

"It is part of the same hay that has been placed in the manger. The manger that will be the bed for the little one. The manger that is holding the one who was born that very night to save the world." I imagined a hundred or so pairs of eyeballs rolling behind closed lids.

"Now, reach into the manger," demanded Candace. "Reach into the manger and touch the Babe." A picture of a Babe Ruth bubble gum card I had seen on *Antiques Roadshow* flashed through my mind. Did she really just refer to our Lord and Savior as "the Babe"?

"Now lift the Babe. Lift the Babe out of the manger," whispered Candace. I couldn't help but peek again. An entire congregation of people simultaneously extended their arms slowly in a zombie-like motion. I shut my eyes and did the same.

"Now reach under the Babe. Feel his bare bottom. Feel his sweet, little bare bottom," Candace said, her voice quiet and soothing, still as hypnotic as ever.

"You are holding Jesus." Three second pause. "Jesus." Five second pause. "Jesus."

"Jesus!" muttered Denny audibly enough for at least three rows to hear. Everyone who heard his exasperation slip out looked at him as he sat there, eyes still close, shaking his head from side to side. Suddenly his eyes opened, and he looked around at the congregation members who were seated in his vicinity. He looked behind him in our direction and weakly tried to convey an apologetic look to Michael. Maybe nobody had really noticed who had shown such disrespect to the preacher. However, the elbow nudging, suppressed smiles, and faces staring directly at Denny indicated that everyone knew exactly who was responsible. Denny tried to do the old cough trick, clearing his throat and then coughing into his hand a few times, as if that was the same sound they heard seconds earlier. Even if this had worked on some of the more naïve congregation members, the fact that his entire head flushed bright red as soon as he coughed was proof that he had actually used the Lord's name in vain. The cover up attempt only made it seem worse. Now he was a blasphemer and a deceiver and someone who disrespected his wife when, of all things, she was telling the story of Jesus' birth. The fact that Denny had to sit through another eleven or twelve minutes of additional sermon until he could beat a hasty retreat made me feel so bad for him that I almost wished the Morelands stood half a chance at beating the editors at their game. I knew, though, that it was a fight they couldn't win. I was pretty sure Candace was unaware of the nail-in-the-coffin event until she saw it in the finished cut. She commanded enough respect from the parishioners that they wouldn't have spilled the beans. Denny certainly wasn't going to fess up before he had to. He might have stood his ground over the purchase of a crib, but he didn't have the balls to tell her how he had accidentally sabotaged their position in the running.

Michael wanted to head for lunch and invited us along as soon as he knew the crew was underway to wrapping things up at the church. He and Jamie treated this lunch as if it was some kind of victory meal. As the number of couples had decreased over the past two months, I noticed a bond had formed between them. They seemed to happily agree on much of the final production results on episode after episode. They shared their mutual intuition about the Morelands not being right for the finals. I was pretty sure that they were in agreement on who was going to win this thing, and I felt a sense of relief that the final showdown was fast approaching. In retrospect, there was no way I could have anticipated what was coming right around the corner.

CHAPTER FIFTEEN – "ANOTHER DEAL IS MADE"

Everything about the pregnancy was right on schedule so it was decided that the structure over the last weeks of *E-baby* would go as originally planned. At the conclusion of the latest episode, when it was revealed that America's vote had ousted the Morelands, it was announced that the next two weeks would have one-hour episodes that revolved entirely around the Karnes' and the Wygants'. There would be no voting until after the second interview week which was when the audience had to make their final decision. Jamie was officially due June 27th, which happened to be four days after the last "regular" episode of *E-baby* was scheduled to run. As testament to the importance that ABC placed on *E-baby* in its line-up, the powers that be made a somewhat unprecedented decision to have a "floating" finale for the show. Everything production-wise would be in place, but the actual finale would be live, broadcast on the day after *E-baby* was born. Whatever show held the 8 P.M. time slot that evening would be pre-empted to make way for the most highly anticipated live broadcast in ABC's history. The media was predicting that *E-baby* was going to be the show to finally knock the final episode of *M*A*S*H* from its distinction as the most-watched series' finale in television history.

Shots of Jamie's frequent doctor visits had been

included in just about every episode. It was no surprise to me that her doctor, hand-picked by Michael, had movie star good looks and probably could be considered for his own spin-off after this was all over. His picture, captured at the hospital or a restaurant or jogging on the beach, was appearing with increasing frequency on the cover of all of the tabloids. Jamie and I also experienced no lack of exposure to the media frenzy. At first it was novel and exciting. However, as time passed and Jamie looked more and more pregnant, she got self-conscious and relied more than ever on Linda to dress her attractively for the cameras. It was an ongoing battle between Jamie and photographers; they wanted to highlight her pregnancy and heighten the visual aspect of it while Jamie tried to face all cameras head-on and belly-on to minimize her, as she put it, immensity. She had no control over the paparazzi and was at their mercy when it came to candid, random shots. I was constantly amazed that no matter what potentially awkward shot was taken of her getting out of a car or bending down to adjust the strap of her sandal, she looked beautiful in every photo printed in the magazines. She was glowing with approaching motherhood.

We still constantly needed to be careful about how she was perceived by the public. It annoyed her at times like when we were stepping out to the corner Starbucks when I wanted a skinny vanilla latte. I got to have what I wanted, but Michael insisted that if she wasn't behind closed doors, she wasn't to drink anything but bottled water or a glass of milk. Some of the trashier rags would be waiting to catch her with a Starbucks cup or anything containing caffeine so they could turn it into a scandal. "Mother of *E-baby* Ignores Doctor's Advice!" As Michael surmised, most of the media strove to portray Jamie in nothing but a positive light because they didn't want any backlash from the millions of readers who had become fans. Any negativity toward the expectant mother carrying the most famous fetus in the world would likely be unacceptable to the masses that purchased their publications at checkout lines across the country. These same tabloids still managed to find room to include stories and photos about the right wing groups and the religious fanatics who tried to organize weekly protests, usually on the day of the latest episode being broadcast. Their articles always ended somehow shooting down the notion that Jamie was the most heinous woman in the country simply for putting a baby up for adoption. I guess, in a way, they had their own balancing acts to perform too. Ultimately, it was clear that they were all pro-Jamie.

Our bank accounts were bigger than ever thanks to the mass marketing of everything *E-baby*. The craze went beyond anything we could have imagined, and we were given box after box of the products. We sent most of it home to friends we knew who had kids because the baby wasn't here yet, and even once *E-baby* arrived, we would have no use for the scads of toys, dolls, diapers, clothing, vitamins, formula, or baby food we had accumulated in the apartment. We never did play the *E-baby* board game that Mitchell delivered one morning when he arrived to take us to the studio. The directions were simplistic, and it didn't look like much fun.

"Who exactly is the target market for this game?" wondered Jamie out loud as she was checking out the box. "Certainly no parents in their right minds would want to have their little kids playing a game where the goal is to have a baby. That's plain creepy. Marketing it to teenagers is a really horrific thought, and it looks way too boring to hold an adult's attention."

"I think it'd make a good drinking game for college kids. Every time you get so many points toward the baby, you do a shot," I said. All I got was a stare of disbelief from Jamie. "I'm kidding," I said. "It only proves how hot *E-baby* is right now. Anything *E-baby* is selling off the shelves."

"This stupid game proves it. We're officially *E-baby* whores," said Jamie.

To appear completely fair, the final two episodes of *E-baby* would be structured identically. Part of each of the final two episodes would be devoted to family interaction, testimonials from the two couples' relatives, and time for each couple to talk intimately with Jamie, asking anything they might want to know. I asked Jamie if she would have a problem opening up her personal life again at this point on television, but she reminded me that we were told to expect this from the very beginning, and she was prepared. Michael assured her that identifying specific detailed information about her two sons or their fathers would totally be at her discretion. My background regarding my marriage, especially Rachel's and my unsuccessful attempts at procreation, had already been gradually exposed during the first few episodes. My involvement at this point was minimal. This seemed to irritate Jamie, but I assured her that I couldn't care less and reasoned with her by pointing out that the only two things those viewers across the country wanted to see were a baby and a "winning" couple. It was so intentional that the Karnes and the Wygants were in a dead heat. I've never been more sure of anything. Informal polls on *Entertainment Tonight* and *Hollywood Insider* backed me up. With luck, at least from Michaels' point of view, the neck in neck race would continue to the very end, creating a frenzied audience tuning in for the finale.

The last episodes were being filmed on consecutive Mondays, allowing enough time for the all-important editing to take place before airing on Friday. I was waiting patiently for Jamie, and I sat on the front porch drinking a glass of orange juice and waiting for a driver to pick us up. I was a little worried about Jamie. She had been really quiet the night before. I had tried to perk her up by suggesting a rousing gin tournament, but she declined. Instead, she sat silently staring at the Game Show Channel watching old episodes of *Match Game*, *Family Feud*, and *The $10,000 Pyramid*.

"Don't they have anything on there from this century?" I asked her. "Like *Who Wants to Be A*

Millionaire?"

"I like the old ones," Jamie responded with a sigh. "I remember watching these when we lived in a much simpler time."

"Wow, you're sounding philosophical this evening," I said. I decided to change direction quickly when it looked like she might be about ready to cry. "Feel free to change the channel if an ad for *E-baby* comes on."

"Oh, I will," she answered. We were both apparently suffering from *E-baby* overload.

The rest of the evening was spent with me being amused by watching Jamie watching game shows. She seemed more like her old self when she started shouting out answers to questions. I joined in, knowing that her real enjoyment came from the thrill of the competition. I tried a little less harder than usual that evening.

I figured it was about time for Mitchell to arrive so I went back into the apartment. I shouted, "Hey! Get a move on. They'll be here for us any second."

What I got for a response was a muffled, "I can't go today."

"Are you kidding me? This is it. We're down to brass tacks. Michael will freak out if you're not there, so let's go."

"I don't think I can go. Maybe you could make up some excuse for me."

"Are you sick?" I asked.

"No. And if I said I was, Michael would just send Dr. Perfect Teeth over to check on me. You can come in. I hate talking through this door."

I entered her room to find her completely not ready. She was wearing a brand new maternity top and an old pair of shorts and was lying on her back on top of the bed covers.

"You're going to be all wrinkled, you know," I said.

"There's a lot more where that came from," was her response. I sensed a mood.

"What's wrong?"

"I need to talk to Michael."

"No. Tell me."

"I will tell you. But I need to tell Michael something, and I don't want to have to go through it twice. Would you mind calling him?"

I got him on his cell phone. He was really good about answering it when he saw that it was one of us. "Michael, could you possibly come over here. Jamie's still in bed, well, on bed, and she wants to talk to you."

"I'll talk to her when she gets here," he answered. "I'm more than a little busy right now, as you can imagine."

"I think you probably need to get over here. She doesn't want to come to the taping today. I think she means business."

"Alright. I'll be there as soon as I can. Do me a favor. Can you make sure she's ready to go? Because if I come over there when I've got a hundred things to take care of here, she's coming back with me." He had lowered his voice to an assertive hiss, just in case she could hear him.

"He's coming, but he sounds a little pissed off. Care to give me a hint as to what this is all about?" My fear was that she was getting cold feet and was trying to pull the plug at the last minute. I tried to ignore my stomach which was feeling sicker by the minute.

"I think I'm getting cold feet."

How well did I know her?

"Now? You waited until now for this?" I stopped there when I realized that scolding her was not going to help the situation.

"I anticipated this a million times," she said. "I've seen the episode of *Friends* where at the last minute Phoebe doesn't want to give up the babies she was carrying for her brother and his wife. That's not me, and yet...I don't understand why I'm letting myself get sucked into this maternal black hole."

"Maybe it is you," I offered. "Maybe there's no avoiding the maternal black hole, as you so poetically put it. Maybe you're not supposed to fight it."

What was I doing? I was speaking with my heart when I should have been going with head only. Michael Olsen was on his way, and I felt I owed him the effort to get Jamie on her feet and out the door.

"Then again," I said, "remember when this all started? You were adamant that you didn't want to raise another child. No way. No how. Has that really changed?"

After a few seconds of silence Jamie answered. "I guess not. Maybe it was the thought of almost having some crazies like the Morelands raising E-baby. It made me nuts."

"You know, maybe you're just homesick. Maybe you miss your boys and that's putting you in this mood."

"It's not a matter of being homesick. We were just home month before last for Little Darrell's wedding."

"Right. We were home for all of three days before we had to be back here for the show. You probably just need to get back home for a longer visit."

Jamie's voice rose. "A longer visit?"

This was exactly what I had not wanted to accomplish. Getting her irritated right before Michael was to arrive was not going to help things.

"Sure. A longer visit? Why not?"

I suddenly remembered the trip home as an overload of craziness jammed into a three day weekend. ABC preferred we fly into Cleveland Hopkins airport. It would be much easier to arrange coverage of our trip back east through the larger affiliate in Cleveland. Vincent insisted on picking us up at the Cleveland airport. He seemed intrigued by the caravan of television crew members that would follow us on our trip across I-90 to Erie. I figured Jamie could use some time alone with Vincent to do some much needed catching up. I rode in a rented van with some of the crew and felt surprisingly comfortable being part of their gang. We laughed and joked for most of the two hour trip.

Jamie was staying with Vincent at Little Darrell's. There really wasn't enough room to accommodate me there, so I agreed to stay where the crew was staying, the new Sheraton Hotel right on the bayfront. I had eaten in the restaurant there a few times when it had first opened and never thought in a million years I would be staying there in a deluxe suite someday, compliments of ABC television. Besides, I was happy to give Jamie her space with her kids. I knew how much she needed to be with them right now.

Because of our circumstances and time constraints, it had been decided that instead of the usual rehearsal and rehearsal dinner the night before, there would be a rehearsal in the morning followed by a brunch. When the crew finished getting everything set up at the church, they returned to the hotel, found me in the bar right off the lobby, and dragged me up to their suite for some drinks and cards. I lost over a hundred bucks and blamed it on the fact that I spent the whole time wondering how Jamie was getting along.

The next day the crew and I met up with Jamie at the Lutheran church on Powell Avenue for the wedding rehearsal. It was to be a very small wedding, despite Jamie's offer to throw them any size wedding they wanted.

"You know, I finally have the money to do something for my kids, and they're getting all weird about it," Jamie said to me as we took our seats in the front pew.

"You raised your kids to be pretty self-sufficient. That's all it is," I offered.

"Vincent thinks my life has turned into some kind

of wild adventure. I know he thinks it's cool. But I get the feeling that Darrell thinks I've lost my mind. I know him, and I know when something's wrong between us. I met Amanda's out-of-town family this morning at brunch, and they wouldn't stop staring at me while we were eating. I knew people might judge me for being *E-baby*'s mother, and it doesn't bother me when its strangers. I expected that. But it's different when it's my own kid and his fiancé's family," said Jamie. "And it was really weird seeing my ex-husband. He was acting strange, kind of like he was meeting me for the first time. I've never felt that kind of awkwardness with him before."

"Maybe he feels awkward because you insisted on paying for the wedding," I offered. "You know, maybe it's a guy thing."

"After all he's done for me, I just couldn't let him pay for everything. I hope that's not why he's acting so distant. I mean, I suddenly have all this money. Little Darrell told me Amanda's family didn't bat an eye when he told them I was paying for the wedding."

"Darrell might feel you showed him up, but he'll get over it. Just talk to him again later."

"Do you really think he'll get over it?"

"Sure. But if he offers to pay for the rehearsal brunch or the flowers or anything, let him."

"I'm really glad you came with me," said Jamie. She looked at me and smiled, and I noticed she cast a glance over to the doorway where Darrell and some of Amanda's relatives were standing. I sensed her tensing up, and she whispered, "They're all staring over here at me. Don't look! Well, look, but don't make it obvious."

"They aren't staring at you because they're judging you. They're staring at you because you're a celebrity," I said.

"I'm a bullshit celebrity," said Jamie. "I'm worse than a Kardashian."

"Everyone is supposed to get fifteen minutes of fame. So you get to go over that by about nine months. Roll with it," I said, trying to tease her into a better mood. "Besides, your kid is getting married. Shouldn't this day be about him and Amanda?"

"That's my point. I feel like I'm ruining their wedding. How can it really be about them when everyone is buzzing about *E-baby*'s mom?"

"Little Darrell understands. All he really cares about is that you're here."

But she was right. Through everything, the rehearsal, the brunch, the wedding, and the reception, the cameras followed Jamie and pulled focus from the bride and groom. While their wedding photographer snapped pictures of Little Darrell and Amanda having their first dance together, they were dodging the ABC television crew as they captured footage of Jamie and me dancing off to the side. I knew it was putting Jamie on a guilt trip and decided to do something about it. I asked the DJ if he'd announce that Darrell and his mom were going to share a mother/son dance. Later, on the way back to L.A., Jamie thanked me for the moment it gave them to finally put things in perspective.

Jamie moved to the middle of the dance floor with Little Darrell. They both knew they were being filmed, but they managed to whisper together and dance as close as they could.

"I'm so sorry," began Jamie. "Did I ruin your wedding?"

"Of course not, Mom," said Darrell.

"Look at your brother over there." Jamie cast a look across the room to where Vincent was laughing with some of the ABC crew. "He seems to be okay with all of this, but I get a sense of you not being alright with it. I wish you'd tell me," said Jamie.

"This isn't the time or the place," responded Darrell.

"Darrell, I'm leaving tomorrow morning, and you'll be off on your honeymoon. I want you to come clean with me. I can take it," said Jamie. I kind of doubt she would have said that if she had known what was coming.

"It'll make you feel bad. You're my mom, and I love you, and the last thing I want to do is make you feel bad," said Darrell.

"Then I'll say it for you. You think it's a bad thing I'm doing, giving up this baby for adoption. I don't know how else to explain it to you. It's just something I decided I needed to do."

"I guess it's all in your perspective," said Darrell.

"How so?" asked Jamie.

"You seem to forget the fact that you're giving away what would someday be my brother or sister," explained Darrell. "But I'm grown up now. I just got married. I don't hate you or what you're doing. By the way, before you leave, Amanda's aunts from Pittsburgh want to get their picture taken with you."

Little Darrell pulled Jamie a bit closer as he and his future sibling shared a dance with their mother. They danced this way long enough for Amanda to have time to dance with her father as well as Little Darrell's father. After she hugged her new father-in-law, Amanda invited me to join her on the dance floor. I was close enough now to watch Jamie put her head on Little Darrell's shoulder. Her son kept dancing with her, not realizing his mom had done this to hide the tears in her eyes from the intrusive camera that was dogging them on the dance floor.

My thoughts snapped back to the present as I heard a car pulling up to the apartment. "Wow. Michael must have flown down the highway," I said.

He didn't even knock. Seconds after we heard the car door slam he was in the room with us. He walked right past me and sat on the edge of Jamie's bed. "So what's going on, Kiddo?" he asked.

I was hoping Jamie would just brush off what she was feeling and tell him it was nothing and she was ready to head to the studio. Instead she started again with her misgivings about *E-baby*.

"I'm having trouble dealing with…" Her voice trailed off. I knew she was having trouble saying it.

"With what?" Michael calmly asked.

"With…relinquishing…*E-baby*."

"It's a little late in the game for that, don't you

think?"

"I know it is. It feels like I'm having a panic attack when I think about it though."

I knew Michael was treading very softly. Michael and I both knew that Jamie had the option of ending this if that's what she wanted. When the legalities were hammered out, it was made clear to all parties that the birth mother would have the right to change her mind up until the actual adoption took place. Our lawyer had pointed out that this was not a surrogate situation. It was an actual adoption and wouldn't be final until the baby was given to the adopting parents.

"What can I do?" Michael asked.

"What do you mean?" Jamie asked back.

"Is there something I can do to make this easier for you?"

"I don't see how you can do anything, Michael. Other than be really pissed at me," said Jamie.

"I'm not going to lie. I'd probably be pissed beyond belief if you pulled the plug right now. When all the details of the show were discussed over seven months ago, you assured me that this was not going to be an issue. I only had your word to go on, and I was okay with that," said Michael.

"I don't want to let you down either. You're the best friend we have here," Jamie said, trying not to cry.

"Listen to me. You know I want what's best for you. I'm your friend. Last night Lili was just saying how much she hoped you two were planning to stay here once the show is over. And I agreed with her.

Our "Hollywood" friends suck for the most part." Jamie sniffled and laughed at the same time, and Michael leaned his elbow onto the bed, over her ankles, so that he was almost lying on his side completely on the bed. I was suspicious that he might be using this move to connect with her emotionally in order to influence her, but I brushed it away. I finally believed at this very moment that he was a good guy.

"I do have a little influence at the studio, you know, with the creator of the show. I think I might even be able to persuade myself to make you an offer."

"Michael," Jamie began, but he stopped her.

"I'm not talking about money. I'm talking about security of a better kind. At least some peace of mind about what you're going to face soon. But first, I have to have your word that this never leaves this room."

We were intrigued.

"What are you offering?" said Jamie. "Tell me and I swear, of course, that no one will ever hear it from me."

"I need to hear that from him too," Michael said as he jerked his thumb in my direction.

"Of course. My silence can be bought," I assured him.

"How about I let Jamie pick the parents?" he said without any further negotiating.

"That's not it," Jamie said. "The Karnes and the Wygants are both great couples. I have no problem with either of them."

"No. I think that's exactly it. I know you well

enough to be almost certain that you're going to go through with this. At some point, and very soon I might add, you're going to be just like one of the millions of people out there waiting to see who's going to get to adopt *E-baby*. You're right, they're both worthy couples. I could care less who wins this. But you're the mom. I think you're going to care very much when it comes down to it. And that's why I'm giving you this opportunity."

Jamie stared at him as if she expected him to continue. When he didn't, she said, "So you're saying we can be part of the shadiest fix in modern television history? I thought you said *E-baby* wasn't going to be rigged."

"You say rigged. You're wrong. I say influenced. I'm right. You know exactly how this works, don't even pretend. It's all in the editing, and you've watched it from the start. I've known from the beginning where we were headed, so in a way I guess you could say I was looking out for your better interests from the start. Not that I'm presuming you'd agree with all of my choices, but I've studied every bit of information we could dig up on all of these people. I can't tell you how many nights I've stayed up studying every little detail about them. I did it mostly because we didn't want some scandal to emerge halfway into this and wind up having the integrity of the show damaged beyond repair. But I also like to think that, in some way, I did it for you too."

It must have been the right thing to say because Jamie pulled her legs out from under Michael's arm and stood up.

"You two can get out now," she said. "I just need a minute to get ready."

"So we're all okay with this?" Michael asked, glancing at both of us.

"I don't think I'll need to take you up on the offer, but at least it makes me feel like I have a little assurance in case either the Karnes or the Wygants turn out to be douche bags," Jamie said, and she began brushing her hair.

CHAPTER SIXTEEN – "THE HIPPIES VERSUS THE MILLIONAIRES"

We arrived at the studio and had to deal with everyone's panic about the fact that we were late on such an important day of filming. The fact that we walked in with Michael was like having a human shield to protect us from the annoyed looks and exasperated comments that probably would have been directed at us.

The goal today was to get the footage of the personal interaction between Jamie and each of the remaining couples. Jamie was ready in no time. My comment about her top being wrinkled had obviously gotten to her. She had changed into a new one before we left. Linda had her change it again so she would better match the set that had been meticulously put together for the final scene between Jamie and the Karnes. Linda had Jamie switch from her stretchy shorts into some tasteful, dressy maternity pants. I had to admire how good Linda was at her job; Jamie looked like a million bucks. There was another complete outfit awaiting Jamie. She would change into it after her time with the Karnes. Again, it was specifically chosen to match the other set that had been constructed for the final interview with the Wygants.

Jamie grabbed my hand and told me we needed to find Michael. I was afraid she was sliding back into her earlier funk, but she seemed full of energy, positive energy. We located Michael on the first of the sets, talking to the set dresser who was asking him a few questions he had jotted down on a notepad.

"What's up?" asked Michael as soon as he saw us.

"How soon before we're ready to start?" Jamie asked.

"Not too long. The Karnes are first, and they just went into makeup a few minutes ago. So you probably have about forty-five minutes. Why?" he asked.

"I was wondering if you could get someone to show me the last interviews between Jenny McCreary and the two remaining couples."

"I thought you never liked to watch the rough cuts."

"This is different. We're so close to the end, and I want to get a grasp on what each of them is all about. Would it be a problem?" Jamie asked politely.

"Not at all. I'll just have Jake roll the rough cut for you. I don't know if you'll have time to get through all of it, but I'll come get you when we're ready for you," said Michael. "Follow me."

He led us to a production booth right near the larger room where we used to watch the rough cuts. He got us situated with Jake who was more than happy to accommodate the parents of *E-baby*. He indicated the play button for us to get started and showed us how we could just turn a master knob to the right to quickly advance the footage, or turn it to the left to back it up. He assured us he would be right there if we needed anything and returned to the machine I assumed he was using for editing the same footage we were watching. He donned a set of headphones, and I could hear the faint strains of music escaping from them. He must have been working on adding background music. The difference between watching footage without music, and then with it, was astronomical. In my opinion, whoever mixed the music into the show had one of the most important jobs in the entire production. If I verified Jake was the one responsible each week for this task, I would make an effort to tell him I thought he was a genius. The background music was the emotional backbone of the entire show.

Jamie and I sat side by side and watched the efforts produced from the past two Mondays. Just as I suspected, the scales were perfectly balanced in an almost imperceptible way. As soon as some little comment from Adam Karnes would make you think, "Uh oh, why would he say that?" I would wait for something negative to escape from the mouth of a Wygant and, sure enough, it would happen. It worked that way for the positive things that would make you view one of the couples in a warm, fuzzy light. Whatever Jamie was looking for, this wasn't going to be much help. The Karnes and the Wygants seemed on equal ground, and we were watching the unedited footage. When the edited episodes made their way to the airwaves, they would be meticulously designed to make the task of choosing a winner even more difficult. An obvious front runner would be too boring. Without a doubt, Michael's intention of

---

making the finale a nail-biter was going to be achieved.

After an hour of watching footage, Michael came in to tell us that they were ready for Jamie on the set. We thanked Jake and followed Michael back to where the Karnes were seated on a couch filled with colorful throw pillows. We shook hands with them, and Jamie was led to the chair opposite Jenny McCreary. Their chairs were arranged in such a way that the two of them would frame the Karnes. It had been insightful of Jamie to describe them as "older hippies". When asked about legacies left to young people today, Adam began talking about his affinity for the music of the 60's and old values that he and his wife had been raised on. They believed in eating organic food whenever possible. They grew a lot of their own produce in their garden. I had not seen Jamie this focused during any of the previous interactions for the show. It suddenly hit me that she was waiting for another one of her "signs". If Adam or Luanne jumped up to the 90's and started singing the praises of Bon Jovi, they would probably have edged out the Wygants. Still, the more I listened, the more I liked these people. They were at ease. More importantly, they truly seemed genuine. I thought of *E-baby* being raised in an environment of peaceful music and an appreciation of the simple things in life. I pictured him a few years down the road, helping Luanne pick vegetables from the garden. They would have these for dinner, seated on giant pillows and surrounded by beautiful tie-dyed tapestries on the wall. These were

209

the kind of people who would instill a love of reading in a child instead of plunking him down in front of the television every night. I wished the competition could end right now, and we'd be done with it.

As Jenny McCreary's voice switched to a cadence that indicated she was about to wrap things up, she spoke to Jamie. "Is there anything you'd like to ask Adam or Luanne before we finish?"

"There is, Jenny," she answered. She shifted in her chair, and I knew she was up to something. My heart started racing. "Have you thought about a name for *E-baby*?" she asked them.

I was relieved. That question wasn't such a big deal.

"As a matter of fact, we have," said Adam.

Luanne added, "I don't think we want to say anything about that, though. We don't even know if it's going to be a boy or a girl."

The sex of *E-baby* had been a closely guarded secret. Doc Hollywood, Michael and Lili, and Jamie and I were the only ones who knew what a sonogram had revealed months ago. It added to the intrigue and mystery of the show, and Michael had been adamant that it not be revealed until the delivery.

"It's a boy," said Jamie.

Michael jumped to his feet, and made a sign with his hands for Jenny to wrap things up. Jenny was obviously flustered, and it was understandable. She had been instructed to never discuss this detail in any of the interviews.

"Well, there you have it," Jenny said brightly.

Something America has been wondering about since we began this journey. A boy. I'd like to thank the Karnes for being here today for our final visit with them. We here at *E-baby* wish them luck. And remember, you can vote for them by calling the phone number on the screen or by texting 'EBABYKARNES' to the text number if you're voting by cell phone."

The panel of four froze, smiling into the camera. Abruptly the hot set lights went out, and Michael immediately strode to Jamie's seat and helped her stand up. "Could I have a word with you?" was all he said. He walked her off set, and I followed right behind.

"You broke a rule, and I think you did it on purpose. We decided that no one was to know you were having a boy until the end," Michael said.

Jamie just looked him in the eye and shrugged her shoulders.

"Give me a minute. Let me think," said Michael. The exasperation in his voice made us comply, and we stood watching him as he leaned against a wall with his eyes closed. After just a few seconds he turned to us. "Not a big deal. We have two choices," he said in a much calmer voice. Again, I was impressed that he had analyzed the situation in mere seconds. He continued, "We can edit that last part out, or we can leave it in. The problem with omitting it is now that the word is out, there's no way this isn't going to get to the press. So, let's say we leave it in. It's only going to generate more excitement. Like giving the public a little taste of something before the big payoff. The last promos for the show can highlight Jamie's announcement that *E-baby* is a boy. I can see it blasted across the tops of the tabloids. 'IT'S A BOY! Reveals *E-baby*'s mom…' Jamie, it's all good. This is actually going to work for us." Michael was smiling again.

"I'm sorry, Michael," Jamie said. "It won't happen again."

"No, it has to happen again," said Michael. "You can't offer that information up to the Karnes and not to the Wygants. I'll see to it that Jenny has a way to approach it a little differently, but she'll get you to the same point where you can tell the Wygants." He made his way back to the set to find Jenny and prep her for the Wygant interview. The Karnes had been escorted to a room close by where they switched places with the Wygants. The Wygants were led to their set and were busy getting their microphones attached for a sound check. Michael and Jenny where huddled at an empty table where he was coaching her on what needed to be done.

A half hour later, everything was in place for the final interview. The arrangement was similar to the Karnes' segment, except Jenny and Jamie had swapped sides so it wouldn't appear to be an exact duplication. The set was a little more sedate, obviously in keeping with the personality of the Wygants. An oil painting hung behind the leather sofa they were seated on, and there was a coffee table in front of them with some nonchalantly placed books and magazines.

The process began again, and I couldn't believe it. By the time the end of their segment was ready to close, the Wygants had me thinking they might very well be the better choice to parent *E-baby*. They were rich people, but they were rich people who were really nice. I had thought their money might be a strike against them because the average person wouldn't be able to identify with them. My instincts were now telling me that voters would want to see *E-baby* have the best of everything. *E-baby* was already a celebrity and deserved to live a charmed life. I knew Jamie was probably going through the same thought process as I was. I couldn't tell if the look on her face was one of confusion or distress. There was definitely something going on with her, and I wondered if she was going to break another rule.

This time it was Jenny who started leading the Wygants down the sex-of-the-baby path. "So, have you thought about names for the baby?" she asked them.

"Oh, of course," beamed Blossom Wygant. "If it's a boy, we thought Reed would be his name. It's a family name. I think it has a strong, masculine ring to it."

"And if it's a girl, we were thinking Rose would be pretty. Rose Wygant. My grandmother's middle name was Rose," added Ned.

Jamie just stared at Blossom and Ned with the same unchanged expression that had taken over her face earlier. Jenny just stared at Jamie, waiting for her to take the hint and reveal the sex of *E-baby*.

"So, what do you think of those names, Jamie?" prompted Jenny.

Nothing.

"Is there something you'd like to tell the Wygants, Jamie?"

I saw the vague expression on Jamie's face turn into what I could only describe as a grimace.

"My water just broke," she announced.

CHAPTER SEVENTEEN – "THE REAL DEBUT OF E-BABY"

All that Michael Olsen could think at that moment was that this was the kind of television that people would be talking about for years to come. It was all he could do to stop himself from throwing his fist in the air and pumping it back down with a resounding "Yes!" He knew pandemonium could break out. Not necessarily a bad thing, but he wanted it to be controlled pandemonium. He signaled to the cameras to continue filming and quickly made his way to Jamie.

Once again I found myself following him. We got to Jamie and helped her to stand. Out of nowhere Linda approached pushing a wheel chair. With one of us on either side of her, Michael and I helped Jamie into it.

"Everything's going to be fine," I said. "Are you okay?"

"Look at this," said Jamie as she glanced side to side, surveying the studio.

Half of the people in the room had whipped out their cell phones and were calling God knows who. The rest were excitedly pacing around, debating whether to approach us but knowing that Michael would want to keep them at bay. The Wygants were holding hands, leaning toward us but apparently were afraid to get off the couch.

Michael turned to Linda and in a low voice told her to tell a cameraman to get over right away with a handheld. He started to position himself behind the wheelchair but thought better of it.

"Why don't you do this?" he said, stepping aside so that I could push the chair.

"Okay," was all I could say.

"Good luck!" shouted Blossom Wygant from the couch. Ned gave Jamie a thumbs-up.

"Let's go," Michael said nodding and smiling at me. "The ambulance will be right outside. Jamie will be on a gurney, and there's enough room inside for you, Jenny, an EMT, and the cameraman. Linda, call the hospital and tell them we're on our way. I'll be right behind you."

I wheeled Jamie toward the exit and it was like the parting of the Red Sea. Everyone reached toward Jamie to pat her shoulder. If they weren't close enough to actually touch her, they waved and wished her luck.

The door to the room temporarily housing the Karnes opened, and Adam and Luanne Karnes came toward us. Luanne extended her arms toward Jamie and was moving in for a hug.

Jamie must have sensed that Michael was likely to halt Luanne's approach, and she looked over at him. "It's okay," she said to him, and I stopped pushing the chair.

"Oh, Jamie, Jamie, this is it. You're gonna do great!" Luanne said and delivered the hug. There was a lot of confusion around us, but I thought I heard

Luanne whisper something else to Jamie as she was leaning over her.

Luanne Karnes stepped back out of our way and put her arm around her husband Adam. They both continued to wave as we made our way out the door and into the studio parking lot. I wheeled Jamie right over to the ambulance. Jamie was totally capable of getting out of the chair and into the back of the ambulance on her own, but Michael asked her to get onto the gurney and let herself be hoisted up and into it. More dramatic, I guessed.

Once Jamie was comfortably situated, Jenny took her place next to the EMT near the front. There weren't chairs for us, just something resembling metal benches on either side of the vehicle. I took my place opposite Jenny, and then the cameraman handed the camera over to an assistant so there was no break in the filming. He climbed in and took the only real seat in the back of the ambulance, a chair that was bolted to the floor and could swivel from side to side. His assistant deftly handed the camera back to him.

Just as the EMT signaled for the door to be closed, Jamie sat up on her elbows and peered over her belly.

"What do you need?" I asked her.

"I have to talk to Michael," she said.

"I think he's probably heading over to get his car. He's going to follow us anyway, so you can just talk to him when he gets to the hospital," I said.

"That might be too late," said Jamie. "You know he'll be on his cell phone while he's driving there, getting the editing guys to start putting this together. I really need to see him now."

I leaned forward and asked the cameraman's assistant if he'd go find Michael. He returned less than a minute later with Michael in tow.

Michael leaned his hands on the floor of the ambulance and poked his head in. "How are you doing? Is everything okay?" he asked Jamie.

Jamie hoisted herself up a little higher on her elbows. "Michael, why don't you step back and we'll get," she glanced at the cameraman's security ID dangling from a lanyard on his neck, "Chris to film you asking me that. How would that be?"

Michael and I both could tell she was up to something, and Michael was perfectly willing to find out what it was. "Fine," he said.

Jamie tapped Chris's leg with her foot. "Go ahead and get Mr. Olsen on camera, Chris," she said.

Chris swiveled in his chair and redirected his camera as Michael took a few steps back and re-approached the rear of the ambulance. Michael repeated his previous movements and greeting verbatim. With the camera trained directly on him, he addressed Jamie. "How are you doing? Is everything okay?"

The EMT and Jenny McCreary were now completely focused on Michael. I, however, kept my eye on Jamie. She seized her few seconds off camera to tilt her head directly toward Michael, and in an over-exaggerated manner she clearly mouthed two words to him. I watched as her lips formed the words "The Karnes". My eyes darted to Michael, and I saw him give her the slightest nod, letting her know that he had received the message.

"I'm fine, thanks. Let's go deliver a baby!" she cried joyously.

Chris had swung the chair back so he could focus on Jamie, and once again the camera was trained on her. The back door of the ambulance was closed and secured, and we were on our way.

Jamie spoke up as the ambulance began backing up to prepare for our trip to the hospital. "Chris, I promise not to deliver this baby during the ambulance ride. Could you maybe turn the camera off while we're en route?"

"Sorry. Mr. Olsen's orders," he said. He shrugged his shoulders apologetically as he said it, an awkward movement since his right shoulder was bearing most of the weight of the portable camera.

"Are you sure?" asked Jamie, giving it once last shot.

"He's the boss," replied Chris. "I don't know if you remember this," he continued, giving me a glance, "but I was the one you crashed into in your kitchen on one of our first days of filming. I'm really glad I might get to be here for the delivery. You guys are great. I think it's really cool what you're doing."

I could tell Jamie appreciated his sentiment, a final affirmation in the eleventh hour that this was all happening for a noble reason after all.

"What were you trying to…" I began, but Jamie grabbed my hand and squeezed it tightly. She closed her eyes and shook her head a little bit. She obviously didn't want to say anything in front of the other passengers.

"Let's wait until we get to the hospital," was all she would say. The EMT was scribbling something on a paper attached to a clipboard, and Jenny McCreary was texting someone.

When we pulled into the hospital parking lot, we had no way of anticipating the kind of media circus that was waiting for us. Michael had stayed right behind us the entire way. He intentionally pulled his car up close enough to the ambulance to bar the hungry press as they clamored to get some exclusive photos and hopefully a statement from Jamie, or at the very least, something from Jenny or me. He jumped out of his car and reached the driver of the ambulance who was just preparing to open the back door. With Michael's nod of approval the driver did so, and we could hear the whirring of dozens of cameras and the chatter of the paparazzi as they began pushing their way to get a peek at the woman in labor.

"Everyone, back up please!" shouted Michael. "You'll all get a chance to take pictures just as soon as we have a path cleared from here to the door of the hospital. Ms. Jernigan is in labor and will not be answering any questions right now. So please, just let us get through if you would."

Jenny and I hopped out of the ambulance, and the cameras started whirring again. The driver and the EMT pulled the gurney out, and the crisscrossed retractable legs met the ground with the release of a lever. Michael led the way as the crowd parted, and we made our way to the door of the hospital. A no-nonsense nurse met us, shooed us in, and then stood with her back blocking much of the glass door in a valiant but vain attempt to discourage the paparazzi. She reached for the wheel chair that she had waiting next to the door we had entered through and rolled it over next to Jamie.

She started to help Jamie into a sitting position. "I'm Nurse Barb," she said. "Let's get you into this chair. You don't need all this right now. I'm going to move you and the father into a room where you can wait for the doctor."

Jamie gave her a smile of appreciation and said, "Hi, I'm Jamie."

"Oh, I know who you are," said Nurse Barb. "I think the whole world knows who you are." She turned to address the rest of the entourage and reverted to commandant mode. "The rest of you can go to the waiting area if you'd like. Or go home."

As soon as Nurse Barb began checking Jamie's vitals, Michael pulled me aside to let me know that as soon as he had a chance to talk to Doc Hollywood, he'd head back to the studio. Not to worry though, he'd be back to the hospital in no time with more crew. I wondered how Nurse Barb would react to more TV people invading her territory. She must have read my mind because she cleared her throat and told me I had five seconds left before she disappeared through some double doors with Jamie and then I would be left to wait with the rest of them. I received a surprise quick hug from Michael and left him so I could follow Nurse Barb. As the doors closed behind us, I saw Michael giving some last minute instructions to Jenny and Chris the Cameraman.

Nurse Barb took us to a room that was adjacent to a row of examination spaces that had only curtains for privacy. Jamie was obviously getting star treatment because we had an actual door. Nurse Barb had her sit on an examination table and asked her a slew of questions. When did her water break? Was it clear? Was she having contractions? How far apart were they? When was the last time Jamie had eaten? "I'll be right back. I'm going to find your doctor," said the nurse. "If anybody comes in here that doesn't belong, push that button right there, and I'll have Bob from security get rid of them. You wouldn't believe some of the sneaky things I've had to deal with in the past when reporters are trying to get in here." She stopped at the doorway, turned, and smiled at me. "You're on guard duty while I'm gone," she said and left.

As soon as the door closed, I pulled a chair over to sit next to Jamie. "Hurry up and fill me in," I said. "I saw what you mouthed to Michael when you were in the ambulance. What happened to letting *E-baby* take its course and leaving the results up to the viewers?"

"I got my sign. I've been waiting to see if anything was going to point me one way or the other. I just couldn't be sure about either couple. I mean, what did we really know about either of them? But I got my sign so now I know how it's meant to be. Everything will be all right."

I could hear some talking out in the hallway and figured we were going to be interrupted any second. "Just tell me. What made up your mind?"

Jamie grabbed one of my hands and squeezed tightly as she used her other hand to wipe away the tears that were rolling down her cheeks. "As we were leaving, Luanne Karnes came over and hugged me." Jamie's emotions were overwhelming her, and she began gasping a little between every few words.

"I knew it!" I said. "I thought I saw her whisper something to you. Come on. I'm dying to know what it was that made you decide to rig the biggest show on television."

"She just said she was sorry she never answered my question about naming the baby. Then she said, 'His name would be Jackson.'"

I knew the significance of this, having heard the story of the big name debate that occurred when Vincent was born. If it was just me, I probably would have written it off as coincidence, but by now I had come to think that maybe there was something to Jamie's signs.

Three hours later Jamie had reached the point in her labor where it was time for her to be moved to a delivery room. Michael had finagled his way into our private waiting area once he had returned to the hospital. Jamie and he were holding a surprisingly calm debate over precisely what would be filmed in the delivery room. I knew Jamie would have preferred no camera at all, but she had signed away that right eight months ago. The hospital had given approval to

ABC for one camera, and Jamie was fine with that as long as it was Chris on the camera and she had some say on final editing. "I've done this twice before. I can be a screamer," she explained. "I know you'd love to let America see the mother of *E-baby* going over the top and freaking out during delivery, but I'd like to have some say in how this gets shown." Technically she really didn't have any say in the matter, but Michael knew it would be counterproductive at this point to start arguing with the irritable, stubborn woman who was about to deliver the baby the world was waiting to see.

It went so smoothly, you would have thought it had been executed by a Hollywood director, which in a way, it was. Chris kept the camera on Jamie, from shoulders up only, when the last contractions started. He occasionally stepped back and changed angles to include footage of the doctor encouraging Jamie, but he never left Jamie's face for very long. She was a trooper, and this time there was no screaming. I assumed there was a fair amount of pain judging from the way she was squeezing my hand. For awhile I thought I might actually lose some fingers, either from loss of circulation or from being twisted like the lid on a jar of pickles. I wasn't quite sure whether she was taking it so hard on my hand because of the pain she was in, or because she just wanted me to share in hers for putting her in this situation. When E-baby finally entered the world, Chris did film Doc Hollywood holding our son up for Jamie to catch her first glimpse of him. It was a beautiful, intimate moment as, as long as you ignored the fact that it was going to be shared with roughly 37 million onlookers from TV land.

In a very delicate meeting several weeks prior, our *E-baby* social worker had suggested that Michael see to it that his mother and child shot happen quickly. For Jamie's sake, the less bonding time allowed, the better. It sounded cold to me at first, but later when I thought about it I knew it made sense.

That moment had come. After a delivery nurse had finished readying him, E-baby was handed over to me. I had my moment with him, a moment so brief it was surreal. At Doc Hollywood's urging I handed E-baby over to Jamie and stepped away to give them their moment on camera. Jamie never even looked at the camera. She couldn't take her eyes off of E-baby. When the nurse lifted him from her arms and began walking toward the door, Jamie's eyes locked onto mine. I think she was refusing to allow herself to watch them disappear from the room. She smiled bravely and focused her gaze even more intently on me. I noticed there were tears in the corners of her eyes. I could come up with nothing other than giving her a single nod when I returned the smile. It was my way of telling her that everything was going to be okay and that she had done a great job with the delivery.

Apparently it was a day for lip reading, and I was getting pretty good at it. Michael, not wanting to intrude on any audio pickup during the filming got my attention with a wave. I looked at him and he silently mouthed, "Congratulations."

"Thanks," I mouthed back.

I returned my attention to Jamie. Now it was her turn. She moved her lips in an exaggerated way so I could tell she was asking, "How are you doing?"

"Fine," I mimed back, touching my heart with my right forefinger when I added, "Happy." It wasn't a lie, but it wasn't the whole truth either. It was the happiest and saddest moment of my life.

CHAPTER EIGHTEEN – "THE LIVE BROADCAST"

The long-awaited final live broadcast was planned meticulously. It made me think that this must be similar to what NASA goes through planning a lunar mission, except NASA probably didn't worry so much about ratings, and they didn't have a celebrity guest host to add hype to their final show. We had Sandra Bullock, carefully selected from the current assortment of Hollywood Celebrity Moms who had adopted babies of their own. Michael had little difficulty persuading her to be the one to announce the winner of *E-baby*. She was a big advocate of adoption and was more than pleased to lend her star status to draw attention to what she saw as an important cause. Not that *E-baby* really needed more attention. The anticipation for the final live episode was off the charts.

Sandra Bullock arrived at the studio with her son and nanny in tow. The nanny planned on staying in the green room with Sandra's son during the broadcast.

Michael asked Lili to attend the final broadcast and the wrap party that would follow. I was grateful for this because I figured it would be good moral support for Jamie if her friend Lili was there. We had arrived early that morning to be briefed on our roles in the proceedings. Despite being a live broadcast, much of the finale would consist of past footage recapping the "journey" as reality folk seemed to favor calling it. Our part would be fairly brief so we just kicked back off screen in some chairs Michael had arranged for us.

We heard and saw the usual opening of *E-baby* on one of the several large monitors in the studio. Watching all of the faces flash by of the couples we had met and interacted with, I felt mixed emotions. It was a short but nostalgic trip down memory lane. As I watched the couples with their names superimposed over their smiling faces, I couldn't help but wonder what was happening in their lives right now. Were they still pursuing their chance at finding a baby to adopt and love? Had any of them given up the notion? Maybe their ordeal in the spotlight had done something to affect how they felt about it. Were any of them being pursued by media hounds that were still desperately trying to squeeze the last ounce out of any of their stories? Some of the writers had debated having all of the couples reunited for the live finale, but ultimately it was decided it would come off as uncomfortable and painful. After all, it wasn't as if they had lost out on a new car or a bachelorette.

The final shot froze on a split screen that showed the Karnes and the Wygants in similar poses on the couches from the filming just days earlier. The red light glowed on Camera One. It was directed at Jenny McCreary and Sandra Bullock who were in front of a green screen so it appeared that they were standing in front of a larger-than-life portrait of the two final couples.

"Welcome!" shouted Jenny. "The journey has finally come to an end for our final two couples, and tonight you will see the results...LIVE!" I'm here with Oscar winner Sandra Bullock who has joined me for this special event. Some of you may not know this, but Sandra has an adopted son and knows the thrill of that special moment in time when you see your child for the first time. Tonight you'll join us as we sit down with Adam and Luanne Karnes and Denny and Candace Wygant, and one of those two couples will be going home with their beautiful new baby. We know it's a boy, thanks to the loose lips of birth mom, Jamie LaRusso!"

Jenny and Sandra shared a laugh as Sandra added, "Let's have a look back at that moment that took everyone in America completely by surprise." Her delivery was so sweet and natural, and I was surprised when I noticed the teleprompter that had provided her delivery word for word. The light on the camera went off and suddenly the studio was filled with Jamie's voice and image on the monitors. We relived the moment. Everyone around me smiled and nodded and murmured when Jamie announced the sex of *E-baby*. All I could do was wonder what the big deal had been. Why were so many people across the country stunned with the revelation of a baby's gender, a baby they didn't really know and would likely never meet? Why were they still watching it and talking about it as if it was something important in their lives?

Michael came over to give us the five minute warning that soon we would be on camera. A makeup person was with him and gave us each a quick final check before nodding her approval.

After the last seconds of the commercial break were counted down there were more trips down memory lane again as Jenny and Sandra recalled some of the funnier and sadder moments of the previous months. As I watched the familiar footage, I couldn't help feeling that each time I saw one of the final couples, I found myself hoping they might still have a chance of winning, even though I was fully aware of what the outcome was going to be.

When the montage ended, Sandra Bullock announced, "When we return, we get to say one final goodbye to the birth parents of *E-baby*. Stay tuned." The network went right to a commercial, and Jamie and I moved into the interview area, parking ourselves into two comfortable swivel chairs that had been added to the set. The lights came up full just before the camera's beacon glowed again and we were on.

Sandra graciously introduced herself to us for the benefit of the Americans who had no way of knowing that we had already met her when she arrived at the studio that afternoon. Her first scripted question was delivered to Jamie. "So, Jamie," she began, "is there any way I can convince you to slip up again and tell us which couple the country has voted for to be the adoptive parents of *E-baby*?" She laughed and leaned in toward Jamie.

"I wish I could," said Jamie. "But even I don't know yet who America voted for," she lied.

"Care to give us a guess?" Jenny chimed in.

"Oh, no. I think the Karnes and the Wygants are both amazing couples. I'm on the edge of my seat just like everyone else," said Jamie. Hollywood had turned her into quite an actress.

"And what about you?" Sandra asked in my direction. "You've been awfully quiet."

"I hate being called on when I don't know the answer," I said, totally off-the-cuff. I was surprised and, I admit, a little pleased when I got a big laugh from everyone in the studio. Despite the bright stage lights, I could even see Michael off to the side of Camera One smiling and nodding his head in approval of my unintentional wit.

"What are your plans now that *E-baby* is coming to a close tonight?" It was Jenny being off the cuff this time. "Where do you see yourselves, say, a year from now?"

"I haven't thought about it much," I responded. "I guess we'll probably find some kind of regular jobs out here. We'll need to finally get a real place to live. I mean a place that's really ours."

"Is that right, Jamie? You've decided to make California your home?" asked Jenny.

"California just doesn't feel like home to me," replied Jamie.

"What? I thought you liked it here," I said, not able to mask my surprise. I couldn't believe I was hearing this for the first time, let alone on national television. Once again Jamie didn't disappoint Michael. She had a way of springing things unexpectedly on the viewers. And me. I felt hurt that

231

she had never even brought her plans up for discussion before this. "I have to say, I'm a little thrown by this. Don't you think you might have mentioned this to me, maybe even in a more private setting?"

"Don't you think you might have told me you bought a car? I figured that meant you had decided to stay. Unless, of course, you bought the car for the sole purpose of having a way to get us back to Pennsylvania," Jamie said.

She had me there. I had bought a car two days earlier, a white Z4 BMW, knowing that soon the driver at our beck and call would be reassigned when the show wrapped. She must have seen the paperwork I had stashed between the toaster and the espresso machine on our counter. My theory of hiding something in plain sight obviously didn't work out so well when Jamie was the one I was hiding it from.

"I didn't tell you I was getting a car because...I wanted to surprise you."

"Well, I didn't tell you I'm leaving because I wanted to surprise you."

"That doesn't even make sense. You surprise someone with a car. That's what a surprise is. You hurt someone by leaving them," I said, forgetting for a moment that we were having it out on television. Not that that would have stopped me.

It didn't stop Jamie either. She fired back, "No, hurting someone happens when you just assume they'll want to keep living in some kind of pseudo reality. And selfish. It's selfish. I need to get back to my life. My real life."

As much as Michael might have loved catching a good fight on camera, we were definitely killing the celebratory party atmosphere he was aiming for, and he pointed to Jenny McCreary and gave her the wrap up signal. Jenny looked like a deer caught in the headlights. Poor Sandra Bullock looked like she just wanted to leave.

"Well, I guess we'll all have to wait to see how this turns out," interrupted Jenny. "But now it's time to see how America voted." Michael began shaking his head violently and pointed to the scrolling cue monitor. "I mean we'll be back for the moment you've all been waiting for right after the break," she read.

The lights dimmed down and Jamie and I retreated to opposite sides of the camera. Everyone else was too busy in preparing for the final segment to notice us. When the lights went back to full and the signal was given, Jenny stood solo in front of the camera. "Can we have our remote rooms on screen now?" she asked, a huge smile plastered on her face. Behind her, again in split screen but this time live, the Karnes and the Wygants could be seen in their separate rooms, seated and watching large screen televisions. They had been watching the entire show so far, isolated in their own private spaces.

Jenny's voice soared. "America voted and we are ready to announce the name of the couple who will leave today with their adopted baby." Ominous music began pulsing as the camera shots closed in on the two couples, four faces full of hope. "The parents of *E-baby* are…." Jenny paused for the obligatory interminable moment of tension. And then, just as Jenny announced their names, the door behind the Karnes opened, and Doc Hollywood and a nurse, or more likely an actress in a nurse's uniform, entered with E-baby. "Adam and Luanne Karnes!" declared Jenny triumphantly.

The music changed to Amy Grant's recording of "Baby, Baby" blasting through the studio monitors. "Baby, baby, you set my heart in motion…" The Karnes stood, covering their mouths with their hands as doctor and nurse approached them with their prize. I have to admit, when Luanne reached out and received the bundle that was E-baby, I had a tear in my eye. Adam put one arm around his wife and his other arm joined hers in cradling E-baby. The monitor now showed only the Karnes' room in full screen. It was as if the Wygants had suddenly disappeared from the face of the earth. It didn't matter since the millions of eyes watching were glued on E-baby in close up.

Michael shouted, "That's a wrap! Thank you, everybody. See you at the party." Hugs and congratulations abounded. Jamie walked over to a chair and picked up the jean jacket she had worn to the studio that day. I noticed she glanced at the *E-baby* logo that was emblazoned on a heavy fabric patch and sewn to the back of the jacket. One of the crew had brought his girlfriend to the finale. She was one of many guests who were allowed to be there, acting somewhat as a live studio audience. They had been penned into an area with padded chairs behind a half wall in the studio that served just that purpose for other shows.

The young woman timidly approached Jamic and extended her hand. Jamie slung the jacket over her shoulder and returned the handshake. "I'm Natalie Arnold, a big fan," she said. "I'm originally from Pennsylvania. Small world, huh? This is my fifth year here as a transplant from the East. You did a great job. I really enjoyed the show. I'm sad it's over."

"Really?" asked Jamie. "Why is that, Natalie?" Jamie asked the question with sincerity and absolutely no hint of sarcasm.

"Well, I feel like I've gotten to know you. I feel like I know you better than I know some of my own friends. I'm going to miss you," said Natalie, as she spontaneously wrapped Jamie in a giant hug.

"I like your shirt," Jamie said smiling. Natalie stepped back and glanced down at herself as if she had momentarily forgotten she had worn her *E-baby* t-shirt to the live broadcast. "You really need the matching jacket," added Jamie as she pulled the jean jacket from her shoulder and handed it to Natalie.

"For real?"

"For real," said Jamie.

Jamie turned and saw me standing off a bit to the side near the place where the crew had rolled the enormous sleeping camera.

"I really have to go," she announced, addressing me and Natalie at the same time.

"Aren't you going to the wrap party?" asked Natalie. "I can't wait. I've only been to a couple of them, but they're always a blast. They can go on for hours."

"I'm not sure if I..." I began as I approached them, hesitating to get a feel for Jamie's take on attending the party.

"Nah," said Jamie. "When Michael announced it was a wrap, I pretty much took his word for it."

"I'm not up for it either," I added. "I think I'd rather be sitting on a screened-in porch having a glass of wine and a cutthroat death match of gin rummy."

"Absolutely," said E-baby's mom.

We couldn't find Mitchell, but a different studio driver on duty seemed visibly annoyed that we were asking him to drive us home. His wrap party plans would have to be put on hold, at least for a little bit.

We sat in the back seat of the studio car, turning slightly to face each other, but we didn't speak on the ride back to our apartment. Jamie's smile looked happy, maybe a little distant. Her eyes looked sad.

Everyone connected to us that day seemed full of emotion. What was wrong with me? All I could think was, "Wow! I got to meet Sandra Bullock."

CHAPTER NINETEEN – "LIFE AFTER E-BABY"

A month later I was waiting on the porch of my modest but very cool rental in Laguna Beach. It was a little farther away than I would have liked, from the place I had called home for the last several months. Michael and Lili lived about halfway between my new place and the studio where we had spent so much time. I was nervous being left alone, but I felt some comfort having them fairly close. I had read Michael correctly from the start and was happy to discover there was no bullshit to his friendship. I had wondered if we would ever hear from him again once *E-baby* wrapped, and I got a rush of good feeling when the phone rang early the very next day and I saw it was Michael calling. At first I figured he was just calling to give the obligatory thanks and good luck speech. He started with that, but then he asked what my next move was going to be. When I told him I was going to hit the ground running and look for a place to live, he volunteered to help me find a place. Because of his connections and his knowledge of the lay of the land, after only three days of searching, the task was accomplished. I could take occupancy exactly three weeks after the show ended. There had been no problem with Jamie and me staying in our apartment for awhile. ABC had secured it for an extra month past the projected end date of the show, just in case there was a glitch in the plan, like Jamie going past her due date. I assumed she would just come and stay with me in my new place for the few days remaining before her departure. She decided she was staying by herself at the apartment. She offered an excuse about not wanting to have to keep packing and moving the things of hers that hadn't already been shipped home. I offered to stay with her until she left, yet she insisted I needed to get to my new place. I knew she needed just a little separation before we eventually parted ways for good.

Michael, Lili, and Jamie pulled into the driveway of my bungalow at 10 A.M. on the morning that Jamie was to leave.

"I can't wait to see this place," said Lili. "Michael says it's perfect."

"Michael has better taste than the rest of us put together. Well, except for me and Lili," said Jamie. She hadn't even been there five minutes and was teasing me already, and I felt a great sense of relief.

We walked through the new place, and I appreciated the oohs and aahs. It wasn't a huge place, but it had charm and character. Everyone agreed that it was worth it alone to have the back patio, a tastefully constructed brick and stone combination that was reached by exiting through French doors in the living room. Half of the patio had total sun, and half was shaded for most of the day by some stately, mature trees. One end of the patio had a permanent brick structure that was part fire pit, part outdoor grill.

"We'll have to grill out here as soon as I get

settled," I said. As soon as I said it, I regretted it. Everyone standing there realized the obvious, that Jamie would be left out of that equation.

Instead of allowing it to seem awkward, Jamie said, "That's a great idea! It's too bad I can't just pop over for that, but it's gonna be a little far."

The afternoon summer sun was brutally hot so sitting on the patio was not an option. We retreated into the air-conditioned bungalow and took the four padded stools that surrounded a countertop island that jutted into the kitchen. I mixed a pitcher of Arnold Palmers in honor of Jamie. Last summer concluded with the Arnie P being the most popular "drink of the day" for at least the last two weeks of Pool Party. I wondered if Pool Party would be started up again and continue without me. It was just one of many things I had thought of that day to make me feel even sorrier for myself.

There was an awkward silence for a few seconds, broken only by the sound of ice cubes being swirled around by plastic straws. Lili broke the silence, thank God. "We're really going to miss you, Jamie. We never even considered the possibility that you might go back East after *E-baby*," she said.

"Thanks, that's sweet. I'm going to miss all of you. But it's what I feel I need to do," Jamie said.

"You're welcome to come visit anytime, you know," offered Michael. "How about coming for the premiere of my next show? I've got two in the works, as a matter of fact. *E-baby* has everyone at ABC chomping at the bit to see what I come up with next. I guess I kind of have you to thank for that." He reached over and gave Jamie's hand an affectionate squeeze.

"Then you'd better thank him too," she said, tossing her head in my direction, "or he'll feel left out and pout for a week. E-baby wasn't immaculate so I guess he deserves a little of the credit." It didn't escape my attention that she had finally become comfortable mentioning the E word. She had conspicuously avoided any discussion of E-baby since the finale had been broadcast.

"Are you moving back to the same place you lived before?" asked Lili.

"No. I'm going back a little more flush than when I left so I figured I'd splurge and go condo. There are some really nice ones overlooking the bay up for leasing. Lorene forwarded some pictures to me. I'm staying with her when I get back, but I expect to have my own place pretty quick."

"Or you could just stay," I said.

Lili started a polite laugh thinking I was making a joke but quickly stopped when she saw the serious look on my face.

"We're not going to have this discussion again," Jamie stated firmly.

"Do you guys want us to give you a little privacy? We could go walk around the yard or something. I mean, we barely saw the outside of the place except for the patio," Michael offered.

"Absolutely not," replied Jamie. "You're staying right here. This is my going away party, and I want to spend it with the three people who have been my life for the last two-thirds of a year."

I wasn't quite ready to give up. "It just sucks that you're so stubborn," I said.

"Me stubborn? You haven't let up about this since you found out I decided to go back."

"Don't you find that flattering? Don't you realize how much I want you to stay?" I felt bad for the condescending tone my voice took on the next line of my tirade, but I was pissed off that she was taking her departure so casually. "I suppose if you got another sign, you'd stay. You're an adult. You can make decisions without having to get some sign from outer space or from God or the Twilight Zone."

"Exactly," said Jamie. "I made up my mind all on my own. I didn't look for a sign. I didn't listen to you. I decided for myself, and you need to accept that."

"What are you going to do when you get back there?"

"I'm pretty sure I'm going back into the classroom. I miss my art."

"Then buy a new paintbrush, but don't go back to teaching." My voice got louder. "I thought you hated teaching!"

This was shaping up to be the last time we would be able to square off in competition for awhile, so Jamie upped her volume just enough to out-yell me but not enough to scare Lili and Michael. "I thought I hated it too!" she shouted. Then in one of her most reliable moves, she squashed me by bringing her voice back to room temperature and turning totally sane and rational. "But I don't after all. I realized that after only a couple of weeks out of the classroom. I want back in, and if I go now, I might still be able to find something for the fall. This isn't me out here. This is you. You're going to be okay. You just need to let me go."

"Remember that discussion we had at Pool Party when your next door neighbor Jack told us he was being transferred out of town, but he didn't want to leave, and you told him it didn't matter where you made your life, what mattered was what you made your life? At the time I thought it was a little heavy on the Hallmark side, but I think it's really true. Maybe you should listen to your own advice."

"Alright, listen to me. I wasn't going to say anything about this because I know we're going to still have the media prying into our lives for a while longer. I swore I wasn't going to mention what I'm about to tell you because the last thing I want to do is drag my kids into some spotlight that would upset their lives. They've managed to stay out of this completely, and that's the way I want it to stay," said Jamie.

"What are you talking about?" I asked, not quite sure where she was going with this.

"Sometimes it is important where you decide to make your life. Mine needs to be near them now. From the start I said I wanted to have a baby but not have to raise it. In a roundabout way I guess I'll get what I wanted from the start. Little Darrell and Amanda are having a baby. I know now what it is I want. I want to be there to spoil that kid rotten. I miss my boys. I don't want to miss them anymore, and I don't want to miss their kids either. Notice I'm not quite comfortable yet referring to myself using the "G" word."

I think in that moment Michael, Lili, and I realized fully for the first time what an emotional toll *E-baby* had taken on Jamie.

Jamie looked Michael in the eye and firmly spoke her mind. "Michael, you know as well as I do that the tabloids would love to swoop in and announce how E-baby's real mom is getting some kind of second prize. I never want to see my grandchild's picture showing up on *Entertainment Tonight* or some magazine cover. I want my privacy back, and I'm hoping you can help me with that."

"I'll do everything I can," said Michael. "You do realize that as long as your face is on *E-baby* products, people are still going to recognize you wherever you are. Of course, if things at ABC go as planned, any day now you're going to see promos for *E-baby: Season 2*. At least that'll take the spotlight off you guys and put it onto the object of America's next obsession."

"Ugh, part of me wants to just sit down with the next nationally televised mother-to-be and tell her what to expect," Jamie said.

"Me too," I added. "I could write a book."

When we got to the airport, I insisted on parking the Beamer and walking Jamie into the terminal. She

243

didn't object. We waited in line, and when it was her turn to approach the counter, I hoisted her suitcase onto the ledge near check-in. I turned to her to face the inevitable good bye.

"This was something, wasn't it," she said.

"It certainly was," I replied. "Call me when you get there."

"I will."

I hugged her for a long time, but it didn't last long enough. "I'd better go," she said.

I walked to the exit and turned to wave to her. I saw her in the distance taking her shoes off in preparation for passing through security. She never looked back. A moment later she had disappeared into the long lines of people.

When I got back to the car I noticed a green shopping bag on the floor of the passenger side. Jamie was the most organized person I had ever met, and it was unlike her to forget anything. I got into the driver's seat and reached over to retrieve the bag. I looked inside and when I saw a box wrapped in bright tissue paper, I realized it was a gift. Taped to the gift was a card. I pulled the card from the gift and set it aside. I tore the paper off to reveal an *E-baby* Game, a new one still in its original plastic wrap. I opened the card, preparing myself for Jamie's parting wiseass comment. The card had a simple beach scene at sunset on the front, very California. The message inside was brief. "Find someone to play this with."

I turned the radio on and made my way toward the coast, not the most direct way for me to get home, but

I was in no hurry. I decided not to look back either.

ACKNOWLEDGEMENTS

E-baby was conceived on a hot summer day at Pool Party exactly as it happens in the novel. My friend Jill Pettigrew and I actually convinced one of her best friends (who would later become Lorene) that we were seriously considering having a baby and selling it on eBay. The joke played out, her friend was assured that we were kidding, but Jill and I kept talking about how the premise might actually evolve story-wise if we had been serious. First and foremost, I need to thank Jill for convincing me that *E-baby* was a story worth telling.

I also need to thank my friends who let me bounce ideas off them. They patiently tolerated phone calls and visits so I could run the latest chapter by them. Their encouragement kept me going from start to finish. Jeff Porterfield, Patty Corella, Ned Smith, Michael Tkach, Chris Reinwald, Denise Arnold, Lori Wescoat, Jamie Grady, John Leemhuis, Bob Bearfield, and my family have my deepest appreciation for their help and support.

I also must thank my mentor, Ray Flynt, my friend and author of the Brad Frame mystery series. When I went to Florida to vacation with him and his wife Rebecca, Ray insisted I bring my laptop and make it a "writing vacation." His advice was invaluable.